Murder *chez* Proust

Estelle Monbrun

Translated from the French by David Martyn

Arcade Publishing • New York

Copyright © 1994 by Éditions Viviane Hamy
Translation copyright © 1995 by Arcade Publishing, Inc.

FIRST ENGLISH-LANGUAGE EDITION

The characters and events in this book are fictitious. Any similarity to real persons, living or dead, is coincidental and not intended by the author.

Library of Congress Cataloging-in-Publication Data

Monbrun, Estelle.
     [Meurtre chez tante Léonie. English]
     Murder chez Proust / Estelle Monbrun ; translated from the French by David Martyn. — 1st North American ed.
        p.   cm.
     ISBN 1-55970-283-4
     1. Proust, Marcel, 1871-1922 — Homes and haunts — Fiction.
I. Martyn, David, 1959-   . II. Title.
PQ2673.O4277M413   1995
843'.914 — dc20   94-39260

Published in the United States by Arcade Publishing, Inc., New York

Distributed by Little, Brown and Company

10 9 8 7 6 5 4 3 2 1

BP

PRINTED IN THE UNITED STATES OF AMERICA

For Al

If I were a maker of books, I would make an annotated register of the various ways of dying....

—Montaigne

1

IT WAS ABOUT TIME the weather cleared up, Émilienne thought as she made her way along the towpath on this unusual morning of November 18. Her back had been acting up again. After countless days of driving rain, sudden rises in the level of the Loir, and an interminable fog, the sun had reappeared miraculously, lining the desolate branches of the trees with a luminous fringe and painting the facades of the village houses a rosy pink. It was going to be a beautiful day.

Émilienne quickened her pace. It wouldn't do to get there late today, what with the convention of American Proustians. But why on earth did they have to pick the month of November? Normally the events all took place in the summer. And there was enough work even then, when she didn't have to deal with the heating and the mud. . . .

Émilienne had been "looking after" the Prousts' house, as she put it, for over twenty years. She knew all the little nooks and crannies, had opened all the closets, and had

1

seen more temporary personnel pass through than many a corporate manager. She was a native of the village, and in her newly renamed capacity as "surface technician" she was paid by the town government to maintain cleanliness and tidiness in the house of Marcel Proust's paternal aunt Élisabeth Amiot, which visitors from all over the world insisted on calling "Aunt Léonie's." She shook her head in disapproval on her way by the wash basin as she thought of the pilgrims who periodically invaded the village, all with the same book in their hands, trying to find the "aroma of Combray," as the current secretary would say. Émilienne had nothing but disdain for the "sickretaries," as she called them, who had replaced each other at the house in rapid succession, each one as useless as the other. The last one was the worst. Gisèle Dambert. An intern, a pretentious Parisian who had brought in a computer and had ordered the lock changed on the room that served as an office. "Don't disturb the office, Émilienne," she would say sharply.

"I really wonder what she's up to in that office," Émilienne would often grumble to the grocer's wife next door.

"You don't think . . . ?" the merchant would answer with a knowing look.

"With all these foreigners, nothing would surprise me," Émilienne would go on, nodding her head ominously. "Mark my words, Mme Blanchet, one of these days there's going to be a tragedy."

So far Émilienne's tragedies had consisted of broken windows, a missing bauble, a tile that had slipped off the roof — all the imponderable little incidents that could make more work for her, upset the smooth operation of the house, threaten its status quo, and require the intervention of the repairmen — along with the secretary, her greatest adversaries. "No telling what she'll have in store

2

for me today," she grumbled as she shoved open the garden gate, setting off the shrill jingle of the old steel bell.

Everything seemed normal. The flower beds were ready for winter. The last leaves had been gathered up by the gardener the day before. The glass door of the orangery was closed. Inside, one could just make out the freshly painted rattan chairs, neatly lined up in rows. The way they get ready for these Americans, you'd think they were all God's gifts to mankind, she thought. But they do bring in a lot of money, I suppose. . . . Her eyes settled on the statue of the bathing girl, slightly askew on its pedestal in the middle of the main flower bed. The plaster, soiled and chipped in places, was lit up unflatteringly by the first rays of the sun. If they don't want the frost to split it in two, we're going to have to bring it inside, she said to herself. I thought Théodore had already done it. They must have brought it back out for the conference. First thing tomorrow, I'll put it back, she concluded as she threw back the bolt on the door to the house with a violent twist of the key.

The usual chill of the uninhabited premises reminded her of her first task: the boiler. She and the boiler were in a perpetual state of war, each of them wondering who would give up first. Not optimistic about her chances of success, Émilienne walked down the stairs to the basement and spent a little over an hour trying to "get the beast to go." Then she started working on the ground floor, opened the shutters, mopped the tiles in the entryway, dusted the furniture. Émilienne felt almost at home, as long as the secretary wasn't there. And she wouldn't arrive before 12:32, when the first train from Paris got in. Apparently there were no other instructions beyond the usual: "Make sure the lavatories are clean." She had time to spare. Weary from her labors and drowsy from the warmth of the furnace and of the autumn sun, she was drawn inexorably toward one of the armchairs in the little drawing room, where she decided to take a rest before cleaning the rooms upstairs. She had not slept well, tossing and turning in a vain effort to ease the ache in her back. She dozed off almost immediately, a feather duster in her hand. From her mouth, slightly ajar, there soon issued a relaxed snore that sounded remarkably like the rhythmic purr of a satisfied cat.

The shrill ring of the phone brought this restorative interlude to a sudden end. Émilienne woke up with a start and cursed the "sickretary," whose silly precautions now prevented her access to the room from which the sound was coming. In fact, there was something unusual about this repeated ring. It shouldn't have been so loud, so clearly audible. Unless . . . unless the door to the office was open.

Forgetting her pains, Émilienne flew up the staircase, taking the waxed steps four at a time. When she got to the top, she saw at once that the door to the office was indeed ajar. Dumbfounded, she wondered whether she dared answer the phone. It would teach that secretary a lesson, but . . . She made up her mind in a flash. She pushed the door wide open and was about to put her hand on the phone when her foot ran into a kind of patchwork quilt with black and white squares. Startled, she took a step back, all the while staring intently at what seemed to be a large cloth dropped carelessly on the floor. Suddenly the scrap of cloth took shape: it had arms and legs and a black wig that lay in the middle of a red puddle. The cloth was a checked suit, inside which Émilienne saw what she took to be a dead Gisèle Dambert.

Horrified to see her most secret wishes fulfilled in such a way and oblivious to the fact that the phone had finally

4

stopped ringing, Émilienne ran down the stairs faster than she had come up and rushed into the street, screaming: "The sickretary is dead! The sickretary is dead!" In her panic, she failed to notice that the door to the street was unlocked.

A few minutes later, she was seated comfortably in the room behind Mme Blanchet's shop, taking small gulps from her second glass of cognac.

"My God, it can't be true, it can't be true," the grocer's wife said for the third time as the game warden walked in, his uniform meticulously cleaned and pressed, his mustache trimmed to perfection, his eyes bright and lively. As children they had often played cops and robbers together, and Émilienne had had designs on him when she was twenty. But he had married a girl from Bailleau. Now he was a widower, and his sister kept house for him. Émilienne straightened up and pushed a rebel strand of gray hair back into the bun on her head.

"So, Émilienne," he burst out cheerfully, "what's this I hear? What happened exactly?"

"What happened? It happened that the sickretary is dead. She's up there in her office. You can go and see for yourself. I'm not going back, I'm never going back up there. When I think that I was downstairs, asl—" She broke off just in time to keep from saying the forbidden word.

"Are you sure?"

"Of course I'm sure. I saw her with my own eyes, on the floor — in a pool of blood," she added, suddenly remembering a fitting cliché from one of the few mysteries she had read.

"All right, I'm going in. Don't anyone leave," Ferdinand ordered.

The few moments he was away were filled with the

incessant flow of Mme Blanchet's useless prattle, which continued unchecked after the arrival of the dentist's wife, who had come to hear the news. Émilienne, as tense as a wound-up spring, kept her eyes nailed to the door of the shop. She seemed to be awaiting a verdict.

After what seemed like an eternity, the game warden reappeared, visibly shaken. He walked up to her slowly. "We're going to have to call Paris," he said in a dismayed tone.

"Paris?" cried Émilienne. "Paris! Why not Chartres?"

"Paris, because it isn't Gisèle Dambert whose body is lying up there, Émilienne. It isn't the secretary. It's the president of their American society, the Proust Association."

"The president of the — Mme Bertrand-Verdon?"

It was too much for her to bear. Émilienne broke out into a cold sweat and felt suddenly sick to her stomach. Her vision blurred, her breathing shortened. Her bony body slipped effortlessly from the chair and would have hit the floor if the warden's arm, still as muscular as in its youth, hadn't grabbed hold of her before she went down. At the age of sixty-two, for the first time in her life, Émilienne Robichoux had fainted.

2

AT THAT VERY MOMENT, Gisèle Dambert was desperately emptying her purse for the third time onto the counter of a ticket window at Montparnasse station. She was sure, absolutely sure, that she had put her billfold into the second compartment — the safety compartment that closed with a zipper. Behind her, people were losing patience. A mother with two children, one of them covered with chocolate and the other crimson with anger, tried vainly to placate them with an ever-more-exasperated "The lady will be done in just a minute!" while they screamed "Ma-ma!" over and over in perfect unison. A distinguished gentleman in a conservatively striped suit with a tie to match sighed markedly. Another, clearly less distinguished passenger said loudly, "Haven't got all day, you know. Think I got nothing better to do?" Finally, having concluded a lecture for the benefit of her colleague at the next window on the disadvantages of the blind hem stitch in shortening skirts, the ticket agent turned her angry gaze back to the pane of glass that separated her from the waiting passengers and hissed, "So?"

Gisèle gave a violent start and strewed onto the floor a pair of glasses, a small powder box, an address book, several pages of which promptly came unbound, and a silver pen that snapped in two. The mother with two children, seeing her bend down to gather up the jumble, gave her a subtle push, stepped resolutely up to the window, and waved an official-looking document: "Three one-way tickets to Chartres. Large family fare."

Just then, Gisèle remembered the shove at Châtelet station as she got out of the metro. The crowd had been so dense. She was surrounded by a group of adolescents who were shouting dirty jokes in Parisian slang above the din of their blaring radios. The stench of sulfur from the subway was as asphyxiating as ever, and in her clumsy rush to get by, she had caught the strap of her purse on the corner of a bench. The obliging young man who had helped her unhook it, and whom she had thanked so profusely, must have been a pickpocket!

Despite her nearly thirty years, Gisèle Dambert was still naive and had never outgrown her childhood shyness. If she came across as haughty, it was merely because she was in a permanent state of anxiety. Always self-conscious about the space between her front teeth, she avoided smiling, and she wore unfashionably long skirts to hide her disproportionately long legs. In her family — a good provincial family solidly anchored in the outskirts of Tours but completely ignorant of child psychology — she had always been number two. Of her older sister her mother liked to say, "Yvonne is the picture of beauty." The picture of beauty had gotten married right out of high school to a medical student who had become a very renowned rheumatologist. They had three perfect children, a spacious apartment in the center of Paris, a chalet near Combloux, and a villa on the coast, not far from Cassis. And they traveled. Yvonne was either just getting back from Egypt, or about to leave for Tokyo, or on her way to meet Jacques in America. She had her hair done by Lazartigue, got her luggage at Vuitton, and bought everything else to match. Radiant, delicately perfumed, she seemed forever to have just emerged from a gift-wrapped box, and when someone asked her what she did for a living, she answered in her melodious and provocative voice, "As little as possible," or, when it seemed more fitting, "Oh, I paint enamels." And it was true. She created charming scenes in shimmering hues that children loved: dolls seated at the edge of a window, tropical gardens filled with brightly colored flowers, exotic animals romping after each other joyfully. Her most recent series had been different. Islands.

Yvonne would never have had her billfold stolen in the metro, Gisèle thought as she left the line and resigned herself to confronting the horror of her situation. For the simple reason that she never takes the metro, added an inner voice that she would never have admitted to consciousness before last night's scene. She glanced at the arrivals/departures board above her. The train would leave in seven minutes. Cheating was not one of her strengths, but this time she had no choice. Selim's name penetrated her mind with such sudden force that she stumbled. Selim would tell me to get on the train, she thought. Mechanically, she directed her steps to track twenty-two, strode past the garish orange of the ticket machines, and chose a compartment in the nonsmoking section of the train.

The car was nearly empty, and she took an aisle seat in order to disappear into the bathroom at the first sight of a conductor's hat. She began to relax and closed her eyes. *Selim. Selim.* Just the name was enough to drive her to the edge of tears — tears buried so deep she was incapable of shedding them.

"Excuse me."

The scent of an aftershave — Eau Sauvage, she recognized it immediately, and in a flash it sent her two years back in time; she remembered the green hue of the bottle, she remembered . . . — announced the entrance of a tall, slender man who sat down gracefully in the window seat on the opposite side of the compartment. He put a book down on the seat beside him, the title of which she could not make out, and opened a newspaper. He could have sat down somewhere else, she thought, vaguely annoyed. There are so many other empty seats, and there he's sitting with his back to the front of the train. She wondered if she should go and find another compartment, but the train jolted to a start just as she began to get up. She stayed where she was. The passenger across from her, utterly absorbed in his copy of *Le Monde*, crossed his legs and gave a sigh that one could have assumed was a reaction to all the bad news he was discovering in his paper.

Somewhat anxious about not having a ticket, Gisèle did not dare to take out of her bag the thick sheaf of papers she always carried with her. Still, she was going to have to reread her conclusion sooner or later before giving it to her doctoral adviser, who was sure to be at the convention of the Proust Association and would no doubt ask her, as he always did, when she was going to be finished with her dissertation. She *was* finished. She had finished it over a month ago. She was going to have to tell the truth about these last four weeks. And about Adeline Bertrand-Verdon. She shivered at the thought. "Chicken!" murmured the mocking voice of Yvonne. "Chicken!" Yvonne had shouted at her a thousand times, watching

10

her pitiful attempts at learning how to swim despite her chronic fear of water. . . .

The man across from her was engrossed in the foreign affairs section of his newspaper. Gisèle opened the latest edition of Proust's *Past Recaptured* to a random page. *It saddened me to think that my love, which was so much a part of me, would be so severed in my book from any particular being that different readers would apply it with perfect precision to what they had felt for others.* . . .

"Tickets, please!"

She had neither seen the conductor nor heard him come through the door behind her. But there he was, standing in his uniform, with a slightly red nose and a face that looked less than friendly. What should she say? Gisèle felt the blood drain from her face. She reached mechanically for her bag and considered playing innocent and lying. She was granted a few seconds' reprieve while her fellow passenger extracted a perfectly valid, neatly folded ticket from his briefcase. He handed it, with an offhand movement of his wrist, to the conductor, who punched a hole in it without even checking the date of validity.

"Madame?"

"I — I don't have a ticket," stuttered Gisèle pitifully under the unimpressed gaze of the conductor, who clearly had heard this line before.

"That's going to cost you a penalty," he sighed, pulling a pad of ticket forms from his bag.

"It's just that . . . I don't have any money. I was late. I thought I could pay . . . when I get there."

The conductor paused. She didn't seem like someone who would lie. More like a trapped animal.

"That doesn't change anything. You aren't permitted on this train without a valid ticket. Can't you write a check? We don't usually accept checks, but . . ."

But she didn't have any checks.

"My billfold was stolen. I didn't have the time . . . ," she said in a tone that seemed curt because of her anxiety.

"Did you declare the theft to the police?"

"No, I didn't have time," she repeated.

The conductor gave an exasperated glance at the ceiling. "In that case, you will have to get off at the next stop. Versailles. In nine minutes. You can go and sort it out with the station master there."

"But I can't do that," she pleaded. "You don't understand. I have to be somewhere. It's a matter of the utmost importance. I'm on my way to a convention. The Proust Association convention. It's part of my job . . ." She felt that everyone was staring at her and that she was submerged in an ocean of disapproval.

"My job, lady, is to root out any passengers without tickets, and you —"

"Excuse me, please." Her fellow passenger had gotten up out of his seat and was opening a suede wallet, from which he extracted a hundred-franc note. "I'm also going to the convention. Allow me to take care of this. You can pay me back later."

Was it because she didn't have any other alternative, or because of the kind twinkle in his gray eyes? Because of the way he looked at her — neither incriminating nor protective, but simply . . . observant? With a brief "Thank you," she accepted. After grumbling about passengers who didn't respect the regulations, the conductor gave her a ticket — with a suitable penalty and a lecture on civil values to boot — and went off to look for other victims.

However unlike her it was, Gisèle looked her savior square in the face. He reminded her of someone. A television reporter? An actor? She had seen him somewhere. On television. A politician. A certain stiffness and an unmitigated seriousness made him look a little like the vice president of the United States.

"My name is Gisèle Dambert," she said with a smile, rather surprised to find herself offering him her hand so forthrightly. "I work on the manuscripts of Marcel Proust."

"Jean-Pierre Foucheroux," he said in response. "I've only just read the first half of *Swann's Way.*"

She looked at the book lying open and facedown on the seat beside him, gauged the relative thickness of its two halves, and guessed, "Sainte-Euvert's dinner party. The first version —" She stopped short, afraid he would peg her as a bluestocking.

"Are you a French teacher?" he asked gently.

"Yes . . . well, I was. . . . I'm writing a dissertation. It's not all that interesting. . . ."

Intuitively, he understood that she preferred not to elaborate, so he didn't insist. In his profession, he had learned to wait until someone was ready to communicate. He returned her smile and took up the book from the seat beside him, but not until he had confirmed his first impression of her with a quick glance. Her black eyes staring straight in front of her, the angle at which her head was propped against the headrest, the engraving on the wall above her: everything made her look like a living representation of Manet's *Repos*.

Unaware of his musings, Gisèle was grateful to him for not forcing her to speak. She would take up the conversation again in a moment. She felt exhausted by the ordeals of the previous night, as well as those that still lay ahead. Outside, the winter landscape of the French countryside, cut into frames by the windows of the train, displayed its shades of brown, gray, and black like a series of lifeless transparencies projected on a screen. Funny how he'd asked her if she were a French teacher. She had been one, briefly, some time ago. In a way, her whole life had been set out for her from the beginning. Even as a child, she would line up her dolls in rows and pretend that she was the schoolteacher, while Yvonne would dress up as a fairy, as a princess, as a "lady." Afterward, the academic prizes at the high school in Tours had led, naturally enough, to the college at Sèvres, to her success in the national examinations, and to her acceptance into the doctoral program in Paris. She had always had to prove to her parents, in one way or another, that she was every bit as smart as Yvonne was pretty. The classroom had always seemed the only place where she would be at her best. If she could just trade in her student's desk for a teacher's lectern when the time came, everything would be perfect. Or so she thought, until the day she found an even safer place: the manuscript room of the Bibliothèque Nationale, the national research library in Paris. It was there, in fact, that everything had begun. And ended.

"Swann is going to die, I suppose," said Jean-Pierre Foucheroux suddenly.

"Not for a woman who isn't his type, and not any time soon. You've still got several hundred pages of him to go," she told him reassuringly — she who had come so very close to dying for a man who *was* her type.

With an assiduousness touching to observe, he went back to his book. Clearly, he was a man who knew how to read. He held the book at the right distance and didn't try to rush. He turned the pages gently, without the slightest noise, at regular intervals. How rare to come across someone who knew how to treat a book properly!

In the Bibliothèque Nationale, once you had gotten past the ill-tempered guards on the second floor and managed to obtain from the librarian — on the rare days when he was neither sick, on strike, or just not in the mood to communicate — the manuscript you had asked for, it was like learning to read all over again, like getting to see what goes on backstage, like plunging into a magic world of enchanted signs where mistaking an *s* for an *n* could have fatal consequences. On pages filled with a tiny script crossed out in a hundred places with black and scribbly lines whose abundance and complexity sent her into ecstasy, Gisèle was able to make out the word "moon" where others had seen "norm"; she substituted "pepper-box" for an obviously erroneous "powder horn" turret; she found an "innerly" that had been usurped by an "entirely." One afternoon her manuscript, thoroughly blackened with penciled-in corrections, caught the eye of the reader seated beside her:

"Are you rewriting Proust?" he whispered in a mocking tone.

She looked up. He resembled a prince out of *The Thousand and One Nights*, disguised as a modern man.

"My name is Selim. Selim Malik. No offense intended," he joked in a half-whisper, offering her his hand. She noticed that it bore no ring and had fine skin and perfectly manicured nails. "Would you care to join me for a cup of tea?"

That same day, she learned that he was a psychiatrist at Sainte-Anne Hospital and was doing research on literary representations of hysteria. That his father had been a Lebanese diplomat, and his mother a French actress who had been rather successful in avant-garde theater. That he was a vegetarian. That he much preferred Corelli to Vivaldi.

It wasn't until later — much later, in her tiny apartment on the rue des Plantes — that he told her about his wife Catherine and their two children.

"We're almost in Chartres, but we'll have a few minutes before we catch our connection. Would you like to have a drink? You look cold."

The tone of genuine concern in his voice did not prevent her from saying no. But to compensate for turning him down, she kept up the conversation, adding, "I was a teacher until two years ago, but for the last several months I've been the assistant to the president of the Proust Association. Mme Bertrand-Verdon. You must know her. She's the one who organized the convention this afternoon."

"I've heard of her, and . . . about her," he said, somewhat reserved. He wasn't lying. He could still hear his youngest sister, a literature student, raging about a spread she had just discovered in a women's magazine: "Another interview on 'Proust and Me' by Bertrand-Verdon. I don't believe it! What a pretentious bitch! And her face! She looks like a witch from Disneyland." Marylis was partly responsible for his being where he was that morning: sitting across from a sad young woman with an impenetrable face, waiting to catch a connecting train on the verge of an adventure that was going to change his life. Marylis was thinking about writing a master's thesis, "Proust and the Women Writers of the South," and when he had joked, "Hasn't it already been done?" she had responded with the critical self-assurance of a twenty-year-old: "Oh, well, I'm sure it has, but badly. The old school."

Marylis had broken her foot the month before in the course of a foolhardy weekend of skiing (without snow!), and her first words when she came to after a painful operation had been, "Oh, shi—! Excuse me. . . ." And a moment later, "This means I won't be able to go to the convention of the Proust Association." Then she had

16

caught sight of him. "Pierre, Pierre," she had pleaded, "don't you have to be in Paris next November? Oh please, Pierre, please, take my place at the convention. You can tell me all about it. Please say you will."

Stretched out on a hospital bed, she had known perfectly well that she could get him to do anything. And he had said yes. And then she had fallen back into a fake but apparently peaceful sleep. But just as he was about to leave the room, she had opened a suspicious eye. "November eighteenth," she had murmured. "Don't forget. . . ."

Suddenly he realized that Marylis would have "adored" meeting Gisèle Dambert.

*

"Chartres! Chartres! Ten-minute stop! Change here for . . . ," thundered the almost incomprehensible voice through an intermittently working loudspeaker.

Foucheroux moved aside to let Gisèle get off first. Was it out of courtesy, or to hide — if only for an instant — his limp? The limp he had had ever since the accident . . .

"I'll see you later, then. For the money," she flung at him, without awaiting his response. He was shrewd enough not to mistake her escape for rudeness.

The wheezing diesel train he boarded had several cars, and he didn't catch sight of her again until they arrived in Illiers. The handful of passengers who had gotten off were all squeezed together at the exit gate. The moment was deceptively calm. Among the people waiting behind the white fence were several women from the village and two policemen in uniform who, seeing Foucheroux approach, stood up at attention.

"Inspector Foucheroux?" the older of the two asked in an official tone.

"Yes," he said curtly, without wondering how they had recognized him. It had been like that ever since the accident. "Inspector Gimpy," people were always calling him behind his back.

"Sergeant Tournadre asked us to come and . . . uh . . . greet you. There has been a . . . uh . . . an accident. He would like you to contact him immediately."

While the officer spoke, the triumphant voice of Émilienne could be heard above the din: "Mlle Dambert. Oh! I told you there would be a tragedy. The president is dead. I'm the one who found her. She was killed in your office."

Foucheroux turned just in time to see Gisèle totter under the effect of the shock and lean against the gray wall of the station to keep from falling. On her ghostly pale face, he perceived a fleeting mix of terror and resentment, but no sign of surprise. A moment later, he himself was surprised by the look of a tracked animal that appeared in the big blue eyes that were now staring in his direction. Royal blue eyes. Gisèle Dambert had blue eyes!

3

AFTER SHE HAD RECOVERED from the shock of the "gruesome discovery," as it was called in the local press the next day, Émilienne found it impossible to keep still. She had made her sworn statement at the village police station next to the town hall with her eyes glued to the clock, begging the police all the while to let her go so that she could get to the train station in time to "alert them." No one understood why she was so intent on "alerting" anyone at the train station, but since she was neither a witness nor a suspect, Chief Sergeant Tournadre did not detain her any longer.

He had already dispatched two policemen to the scene of the crime to keep out any intruders and had reported everything to his superiors in Chartres, who had given him strict orders to sit and wait. It wasn't every day that he had a murder on his hands. He was used to dealing with domestic quarrels, fights that had broken out among drunken teenagers, traffic accidents, and an occasional suicide, but there had been nothing really serious since last July, when the Favert boy had shot and killed his young wife in a well-founded fit of jealousy.

Bernard Tournadre sighed. They were not going to leave him in charge for very long, that was sure. They were going to saddle him with the national crime squad and its cohort of specialists, who would descend on him from Versailles like poverty on the third world. They would already have alerted the D.A. He was not surprised when the receptionist buzzed him and said that the head of the crime squad was on the line and wished to speak with him. They had met once at an awards ceremony, and he had seen his face often enough since then in the newspaper and on television whenever an important case came up. The voice on the line was friendly, commanding, and distinguished:

"Hello, Tournadre? Vauzelle. How are you? Tricky case we've got here. You know of course that Mme Bertrand-Verdon was a close friend of the wife of the minister of culture. . . . That's right. . . . So this is going to require a lot of tact on our part, if you know what I mean. And with all these Americans, we have to be careful not to set off some diplomatic incident that would get the Office of Foreign Affairs involved. We've got problems enough as it is, what with the GATT treaty, believe me! By the way, where are those Americans? At the Old Mill Inn? Good, good. Can you make sure they stay there for the moment? Oh, and Tournadre, not that I want to tread on your toes, but one of my men is already on his way. Completely by chance. I happen to know that he was going to this Proust convention because we had dinner together yesterday evening. His name is Foucheroux. Chief Inspector Jean-Pierre Foucheroux. I'd like you to have someone meet him at the station and ask him to call me on the hot line. He has the number. I'm counting on you, Tournadre. . . ."

Sergeant Tournadre put down the phone, gave another sigh, and sent Corporal Duval and his assistant to meet the unfortunate chief inspector, who was still blissfully ignorant of the Pandora's box that destiny had in store for him. He already felt sorry for the man. Foucheroux. The name sounded vaguely familiar. One of Vauzelle's favorites, no doubt, which in this case actually meant something, since the head of the crime squad was reputed to be a man of great integrity — a rare thing in the police force, especially at so high a rank.

But it was respect, not sympathy, that Jean-Pierre Foucheroux elicited when he walked into the police station at eighteen minutes to one. He introduced himself courteously, apologized for having to use the phone straightaway and in private — as his orders called for — and thanked Sergeant Tournadre heartily for accommodating him.

Ten minutes later he emerged to announce in an affable but firm tone, "Gentlemen, I have just been asked to lead the investigation. I know I can count on your generous assistance. We all want to wrap this case up as best and as quickly as we can. If there are no objections, I would like to call in the specialists straight away and to contact the Office of Criminal Records. Who is the medical examiner? How many detectives can we call on to carry out the preliminary questioning?"

*

"He's a nice guy, this chief inspector is, for a Parisian," Corporal Duval said to his assistant as they were going out. "Not at all pretentious. Very efficient, too."

"Oh, he's no Parisian," Plantard shot back. "I've got an ear for that sort of thing. I'll bet you anything he comes from around Bordeaux. I go there every summer to get my year's supply of wine, and I can recognize the accent. That's where I get my Pécharmant '75 — your favorite," he added with a knowing wink.

*

Alone with Bernard Tournadre, Jean-Pierre Foucheroux took a moment to put the sergeant completely at ease. They soon discovered they had a mutual friend, Chief Inspector Blazy, stationed in the south of France.

"A real pro in rugby," the sergeant said admiringly.

"You can say that again. I had the bad luck once of playing on the opposing team," Inspector Foucheroux said with a smile. Then, in a more serious tone: "I won't keep you much longer. It's lunchtime. I just need to ask you a few questions about the Proust Association before I go and see the scene of the crime."

"Go right ahead," Bernard Tournadre answered amicably. "Although," he hastened to add, thinking of the gratin Dauphinois his wife had cooked up for lunch and glancing unconsciously in the direction of his stomach, the prodigious girth of which betrayed his penchant for the pleasures of the table, "the mayor could tell you a lot more than I. He's the one who takes care of all that, and of the Tourist Office as well." He paused briefly. "He's not much of a team player, at least where I'm concerned. . . ."

Sensing an old political rivalry, Inspector Foucheroux steered the conversation onto more neutral terrain. "Do you often have weather like this in November?"

"No, very rarely. It's what the Americans call Indian summer, I believe. Oh! the Americans! They're staying at the Old Mill Inn, did they tell you?"

"No, not really. I know that the convention is meant to

begin at five, at Aunt Léonie's. According to the program, there are three lecturers —"

"That's right. One of them is at the Old Mill. Guillaume Verdaillan. He arrived here yesterday, along with the first contingent of participants, about twenty of them. The others are coming by bus from Paris today. University professors, for the most part, if I understood correctly."

"And Mme Bertrand-Verdon?"

"I saw her yesterday. But I'm not sure whether she intended to go back to Paris or spend the night at the Old Mill. She could do the drive from Paris and back again without stopping. In her sports car. A white Alfa Romeo." Detecting a touch of envy in his colleague's voice, Inspector Foucheroux raised his eyebrows, expecting Tournadre to elaborate. Which he did, after a brief pause. "I really didn't know her at all. But, just between you and me, she wasn't much liked around here. She thought of herself as God's gift to mankind. People said she was only interested in getting her picture in the paper with one famous person after another. . . . And the way she treated her poor secretaries . . . She tried to get elected to the town council, but it didn't work. Anyway, the mayor could help you on that more than I can. . . . Do you want me to give him a call?"

"Why don't you do just that?" said Foucheroux, suspecting that the sergeant would take a malicious delight in tearing the mayor away from a sumptuous midday meal while recovering the right to go and enjoy his own lunch in peace.

"Hello, Marie-Claire?" The satisfied smirk on Tournadre's face as he spoke into the phone told the inspector he had guessed right. "It's Bernard. Is François there? He is? Perfect. I have a chief inspector from Paris in my office who needs to speak to him with the utmost urgency. . . .

23

Hello, François? Sorry to disrupt your lunch hour this way, old boy, but . . ."

A few minutes later Jean-Pierre Foucheroux was dropped off at the gate of a pretty house with a pink roughcast facade and a garden that stretched to the banks of the Loir. A young girl with a white starched apron, standing in the doorway, told him he was expected in the drawing room.

After the bleakly rustic interior of the police station, the room into which he was shown, warm with the radiant heat of an open fire and papered in a cheerful blue-and-white-striped pattern, seemed to him to be as inviting as its two occupants were tense and distant. "François Delaborde, deputy and mayor," announced rather bluntly a tall, robust man with bushy eyebrows, casually dressed in a turtleneck sweater and a pair of dark green corduroy trousers. "My wife, Marie-Claire," he added almost reluctantly, gesturing toward a small, plump, and lively brunette, wearing a pale blue angora dress and smelling sweetly of lavender. "We don't quite understand how we can help you, Inspector."

"François —," his wife whispered scoldingly. "May I get you a cup of coffee, Inspector?" she said out loud, a hint of a southern accent in her voice. She was clearly intent on keeping up appearances. It was obvious to Foucheroux that the couple had just been having a fight.

"Yes, thank you," he said heartily, purely to fulfill the requirements of social convention. He preferred to drink espresso and was generally aghast at what was served under the generic term of "coffee." In this case, his skepticism was misplaced. The frothy brown beverage that Marie-Claire Delaborde served him without sugar in a lovely Limoges cup was excellent. These people really knew how to live. "Sergeant Tournadre thought you might be able to tell me something about the Proust Association and about Mme Bertrand-Verdon," he began. He saw Mme Delaborde's fleshy hand stiffen in its grasp on the handle of the coffee pot.

"We scarcely knew her," the mayor asserted. "We saw her at the official functions, and that was it. Her death puts the Proust Association in real difficulty. She was the association's founder."

"And what exactly was its purpose?"

"Oh, to attract Anglo-Saxon tourists, to sponsor international meetings. It wasn't a bad idea for the region. It was good publicity."

"It was good publicity mostly for Adeline Bertrand-Verdon," Mme Delaborde blurted out, incapable of containing herself any longer. "It allowed her to travel about and show off at the expense of the taxpayers —"

"Marie-Claire, please," her husband pleaded.

"The inspector has the right to know —"

"It is true that Mme Bertrand-Verdon did on occasion reveal a touch of ostentation that was not to everyone's taste," the mayor set in. "But she was the heart and soul of the Proust Association. She got the minister of culture to agree to come to the convention — he's due in at four, although I haven't heard anything — as well as the renowned Parisian literary critic, Max Brachet-Léger. Surely you've heard of him. He's the one who refused to appear on the television show, *Apostrophes*."

"Is he here?" asked the inspector.

"No, he lives in Paris. He'll just come down for the convention itself, I would think."

"Who else was here yesterday?"

"Aside from the Americans, there was Professor Verdaillan of the University of Paris at Neuilly; a senior editor at Martin-Dubois Press who's also a member of the association's board of directors — what's his name again?"

"Philippe Desforge," his wife reminded him.

"Philippe Desforge, that's it. Then there was the Viscount of Chareilles, who is a personal friend of Mme Bertrand-Verdon; and Gisèle Dambert, the secretary."

"I met her this morning on the train," said Foucheroux.

"A real saint," Marie-Claire Delaborde broke in, defying a warning glance from her husband. She was interrupted momentarily when the young housekeeper came in to summon the mayor to the phone for a call from Paris. "A saint," she resumed as soon as her husband had left the room. "Excuse me for speaking so frankly, Inspector. But Mme Bertrand-Verdon was a pretentious social climber who would stop at nothing to have her way. Everyone knows that she got this sinecure of a presidency by —" She blushed. "By employing means that, well —"

"I understand entirely, madame, and I'm grateful for your frankness," the inspector said encouragingly.

"Take today's convention, for example. The pretext is to commemorate the death of Marcel Proust. But in reality it's just a means for Mme Bertrand-Verdon to use government and university funds to promote her *Guide of the Perfect Proustian.*"

"*Guide of the Perfect Proustian?*" he said uncomprehendingly.

"Oh, so you're not familiar with that masterpiece of scholarship?" she said with an ironic smirk. "We were given two copies. Do let me give you one —"

Just then her husband reappeared with a worried look on his face. "The minister will not be joining us. The inau-

26

guration of a memorial plaque has detained him longer than expected at Fontainebleau."

"Not to mention the time he'd lose on the way here, what with all the farmers' demonstrations blocking the roads. What a pity!" Mme Delaborde said jokingly.

"Marie-Claire, really —"

Foucheroux sensed that it was time for him to leave. "Thank you, Mayor Delaborde, for taking the time to meet with me. And you, madame, for this delicious coffee. It's time I went to the scene of this unfortunate incident to see what we can come up with."

"Let me first fetch what we were just talking about," Marie-Claire said with a smile.

The mayor accompanied the inspector to the door. "I hope my wife hasn't been filling your ears with her stories," he said, visibly embarrassed. "She tends to run on —"

"She runs on in a most delightful manner, and she's been enormously helpful," the inspector responded, a bit testily.

"Here it is," Marie-Claire sang out when she reappeared, holding up a slender volume with a sumptuously illustrated jacket. "It doesn't take long to read. Some pretty pictures and a few quotations. Even François wouldn't contradict me there," she added maliciously. And she slid her arm under his in a sign of truce.

4

WHEN HE CAME WITHIN SIGHT of Aunt Léonie's house, a grayish edifice on the corner of two very unremarkable streets, Foucheroux could scarcely believe his eyes. How could such an insignificant, ugly building have become one of the meccas of French literature? But he had not come to marvel at the transformative powers of a great novelist's imagination. The immobile silhouette of the officer guarding the front door reminded him of the distressing task that lay ahead of him.

Foucheroux had never gotten used to the feeling of nausea that came over him just before he had to enter, once again, the scene of a violent death. His repulsion had increased since the tragic accident three years earlier that had killed his wife. The accident that was his fault. That he would never forgive. And that his body would never forget. The steel pins grafted onto his left knee and the limp that had earned him the nickname "Inspector Gimpy" would never let him forget it in any event. He wondered whether the time he had just spent questioning Tournadre and the mayor had not in fact been a mere stalling tactic on his part, designed to postpone the inevitable moment when he would have to lean down over the corpse of Mme Bertrand-Verdon. He should have insisted at the station that he be brought directly to the scene of the crime.

After questioning the guard to make sure that no one had entered the premises since the game warden left, he glanced rapidly at the rooms downstairs: a tiled entryway, an old-fashioned kitchen, a dining room, and a living room in the fin-de-siècle style of the petit-bourgeois . . . all extraordinarily humdrum, up to and including the door with the red-and-blue stained glass that opened onto an ordinary-looking little garden centered around an imitation statue. He went up to the second floor.

Nothing in the office seemed to have been disturbed since the cleaning woman had made her mad dash out. Automatically he made a mental note of the two windows, the numerous closets, the marble fireplace with a mirror above it on the wall, and the alcove lined with bookshelves. On the large oak desk in the middle of the room was an old black telephone and a brand-new computer. And a key ring.

Between the desk and a green armchair that had seen better days, the body of Adeline Bertrand-Verdon was sprawled in its grotesque position on the floor. Her body looked like an enormous rag doll that a cruel child had dropped and abandoned: one leg bent awkwardly over the other, her face buried beneath a mass of black hair, matted hideously on the right side. Leaning down, Foucheroux observed an expression of defiance and disbelief in her wide-open eyes that seemed strangely to fit in with the grin frozen onto her painted lips. She must have been in the midst of a scathing retort when death struck her down. When someone struck her down.

Although the medical examiner would have the final say, the inspector estimated on the basis of the rigor mortis that death must have ensued about twelve hours earlier, and that it had been caused by a violent blow to the right temple with the proverbial blunt object. He had just noticed a sort of fine white powder mixed into the clotted blood on the floor when the silence of the house was broken by the noise of men's voices and footsteps on the stairs, signaling the arrival of the team from the Criminal Records Office.

A short, bald man with gold-framed glasses that looked as though they were constantly about to slip off his pointed nose walked in and introduced himself exuberantly. "Doctor Meynadier. So what have we got here, Inspector?"

"The body of the president, it seems."

"*Mors etiam saxis venit,*" murmured the doctor. "Well, I'll let our colleagues here take their pictures, and then I'll take a look myself." For the next few moments the blinding flashes and the clicking of the cameras turned the room into a grotesque parody of a movie studio. Carefully, methodically, a lab technician lifted fingerprints, shaking his head from time to time in discontent. Finally the medical examiner was free to examine the body, around which a line had been traced in chalk to mark its position. Kneeling on the floor, he felt the victim's wrist, probed the base of her neck, muttered two or three "ah-hah's," turned her head, which was soaked in blood, to the side, and, the woman's neck twisted awkwardly in his direction, peered at length into her face before closing the eyes that saw no more.

"What do you think?" Foucheroux asked when the examiner stood up.

"We'll know more after the autopsy, of course, but I'd say that death must have occurred at about ten or eleven o'clock last night. The apparent cause was a fracture of the temporal bone, just above the parietal bone —"

"Caused by what?"

"Oh, well, that's your specialty, Inspector. A blunt object, no doubt. The blow must have been struck with great force, and death must have been instantaneous. Nevertheless," he added, scratching his head, "it wouldn't surprise me if we found traces of a toxic substance."

"You think she was drugged?" the inspector asked, clearly surprised.

"I can't say with any degree of certainty, not on the basis of what I can see here. We'll have to wait for the results of —"

"When will you have them?" Jean-Pierre Foucheroux broke in before the doctor could finish his sentence.

"I can understand your impatience," replied the examiner placidly. "As quickly as possible. We're working on orders from Paris, and we'll get to it first thing. Shall we say tomorrow, by late morning? Will that do?"

Foucheroux gave him a wry smile. "I suppose it will have to do, won't it? . . . Did you notice that white powder on the floor?"

"Yes, I did," the doctor replied, rubbing his finger against his thumb. "If you ask me, it's plaster."

"Plaster?"

"Wouldn't surprise me. We'll be able to tell you for sure tomorrow, along with everything else."

"Thank you, doctor," said Foucheroux. "I expect I'll be staying at the Old Mill Inn, but you can always reach me through the police station in the village. Call me at any hour of the day or night, as soon as —"

"Of course," said the doctor, who was used to such requests. "And good luck. Are you ready, gentlemen?"

The officers from the Criminal Records Office were finished. All that was left to do was transfer the body to the morgue and notify the victim's family. And to make some quick decisions about the day's course of action. But before he could do that, Foucheroux would have to talk with Gisèle Dambert. And reserve a room at the Old Mill Inn, where he would set up his headquarters.

But where was Gisèle Dambert?

Before leaving the house, which had now settled back into its original silence, Foucheroux went to see the room where Marcel Proust had slept as a child, striving vainly to reconcile the lush passages that had so dazzled him during his recent reading of *Swann's Way* with the petty reality of the room in which he stood. What a disappointment! Everything was smaller; the magic lantern was a sadly battered gadget; the curtains were faded; the bed was jammed into an unappealing little alcove. He walked to the other side of the hall, but here too he couldn't bring his mental images of Aunt Léonie's bedroom to coincide with what he now saw. Although he could pick out the objects mentioned in the text — the dresser, the table, the armchair, the prie-dieu — he could find no trace in this country room of *those myriad scents that emanate from virtues, wisdom, customs — from a secret, invisible, superabundant moral life hovering in the air* that he had inhaled, it seemed, while reading *Combray*. As he walked over to the bed, it occurred to him that his position at the outset of this case was like that of an uninformed reader who has no idea of how the plot is going to unfold. He would have to interpret signs, ask questions, make searches, reconstruct events, question the accuracy of what he had already learned, proceeding all the while in constant danger of making a wrong judgment.

He gazed distractedly out the window. On the sidewalk across the street, Gisèle Dambert stood looking at the ground, trying to make up her mind what to do next. Foucheroux sprinted down the stairs rather too precipitously for his bad leg, which protested with a sharp, warning pang, but he was afraid she would get away from him. He was wrong. She was already walking up to the door when he tore it open and rushed out.

"I was waiting for you," she said matter-of-factly.

5

GISÈLE WOULD NOT HAVE BEEN ABLE to say what had provoked the spell of dizziness that had come over her at the station, and which had doubtless been caused by the combined effects of a sleepless night, the shock of hearing Émilienne's news and discovering in the same instant that Jean-Pierre Foucheroux was a police detective, and the sudden realization that the events of the previous day now put her in imminent danger.

In an unusual gesture of kindness, Émilienne had taken her by the arm and tried to comfort her. "You've gone white as a sheet, Mlle Dambert. Don't you feel well? Here, why don't you sit down for a moment on this bench. . . ." Gisèle, dumbstruck, had obeyed without a word. But as soon as they had sat down, Émilienne resumed her tale as glibly as ever. "Oh! I can't tell you what a shock it gave me to find . . . at first I thought it was you." She shivered at the thought. "And what are we going to do this afternoon? The police are all there. We won't be able to hold the conference at the Prousts' house."

Gisèle slumped down still lower on the bench, prompting Émilienne to ask, "Would you like to go and get something to drink at the Café de la Gare?" For all the world, Émilienne could not have brought herself to say "at the Hôtel de Guermantes," as the old establishment had been pompously renamed. But Gisèle was not in the mood for playing around with nomenclature. "No thanks," she managed to say. "I would prefer . . . to walk a little."

"To walk, in the state you're in?" said Émilienne with a disapproving scowl.

"Yes, I would like to walk a little," Gisèle said again. "If you would just keep an eye on my bag?" she added, afraid she would offend Émilienne unless she found some way of accepting the woman's help.

Émilienne finally agreed, but only on condition that Gisèle promise to eat something. Gisèle promised, got up, and without thinking, turned into the avenue de la Gare, a broad boulevard lined with somber linden trees. She took a right at the first intersection into the walkway that slopes gently down the hill and past a few ruins to the banks of the Loir, where she wound up on the narrow path that runs alongside the river for a way before opening out onto the rue des Vierges. She didn't even glance at the little flower gardens, whose mossy old stone walls she liked so much to see, nor at the stepped landscape of slate and tile roofs sloping upward to her left like a kind of red-and-gray mosaic suspended in the sky around the tower of the church. Hunched forward, her eyes cast down, shivering in her wool coat despite the mild day, she walked straight ahead until she was standing in front of the Pré Catelan. She pushed open the wooden gate, went up the path that leads to the Archers' Pavilion, and at the top of the hill collapsed onto one of the cold steps in front of the little hexagonal structure.

She had no idea what had caused her to seek refuge here rather than somewhere else. Everything seemed so reassuringly normal: the calm reflection of the pigeon house with its green trellises in the little pond down below, the whisper of the wind in the naked branches of the poplars in the Bois Pilou. Gisèle struggled to fight back the tears that came to her eyes, to control her breathing, to think.

On the one hand, if she told the police about the substance she had put last night into the rose-petal jam that Adeline Bertrand-Verdon ate every evening, she would also have to explain why she had done so and confess where and how she had spent the night. On the other hand, she needed an alibi. It was just as necessary that she hide certain facts as it was that she reveal what she knew. Her life was at stake.

Gisèle closed her eyes and leaned her head against the brick wall. A parade of images passed through her mind. She had to straighten so many things out before she could make a decision. She concentrated on the events that had led her to this place and time. The whole adventure with Selim had grafted itself like an ugly weed onto her privileged relationship with Évelyne. Évelyne . . . For three whole years they had seen each other almost every day.

She would never forget their first chance meeting, late one afternoon in the Bibliothèque Nationale. Gisèle had gone out of the Manuscript Room at about the same time as a very elderly lady with white hair in perfectly set curls and sparkling, periwinkle-blue eyes. Her baggy checked greatcoat and her cane with its silver knob made her look like she had just stepped out of some English mystery novel. The two of them had barely come up to the top of the staircase when, without warning, the knees of the old lady had buckled. Her cane hurtled down the marble stairs with a great racket, and in a grotesque pirouette she swung around on her toe and, unable to regain her balance, tumbled head over heels down the stairs. Her heart pounding, Gisèle flew down the stairs after the little twirling silhouette. They reached the bottom at about the same time. Gisèle held out a rather shaky but solicitous hand and stammered, "Let me help you —"

"Thank you, miss, I think I can manage," said the old lady in a very dignified voice. "No broken bones, I think," she added bravely as she got back on her feet.

"But you've hurt your hand," insisted Gisèle, who had seen a small trickle of blood run down the woman's frail fingers, which were somewhat twisted with age.

"Oh, it's nothing at all, I assure you. It's just a scratch."

As soon as he had seen that he was not in the least danger of becoming involved, a library clerk who had clearly observed the fall came over to where they were standing. "You should go to the emergency room," he told her.

"He's right. One never knows, really, after a fall," added Gisèle. "Please let me accompany you. My name is Gisèle Dambert."

"And mine is Évelyne Delcourt. You're much too kind. I'm sure I can take a taxi."

But Gisèle could be very persuasive when she wanted to. She felt as though fate had assigned her the task of making sure this elderly stranger got home safely.

"I'm afraid that Katicha will start to worry if I'm late getting back," Gisèle heard the woman say in her dignified soft voice. The name conjured up in Gisèle's mind the image of an old Russian princess, perhaps crippled, waiting impatiently in an apartment filled with mementos from the time of the czars for her friend to return.

"Perhaps we could phone her," Gisèle suggested.

Évelyne Delcourt broke into a crystalline laugh that

made her suddenly look a half century younger. "I don't think she'll answer. She can open doors, jump out windows, and let you know with a single glance what mood she's in, but she can't use the telephone. Katicha is a blue Persian cat."

Nowadays Katicha let the world know about her various — and numerous — moods in Gisèle's apartment on the rue des Plantes. Even though their first meeting had been such a failure. After persuading Évelyne to get her wound stitched up by a competent surgeon, Gisèle had accompanied her to her home on the place Notre-Dame-des-Victoires. Katicha had scuttled under the sofa, refusing to show the intruder so much as a whisker tip. But that day had marked the beginning of a great friendship between the old lady and the young woman. Gisèle was soon visiting Évelyne regularly in her home, where they would drink tea, chat, listen to music. Unlike most people her age, Gisèle felt entirely comfortable with the elderly. She liked to listen to them recount their memories of a forgotten time. She liked the sound of Évelyne's voice; and Évelyne, who had taught piano at the Paris Conservatory, had moved in all sorts of artistic circles. And she knew how to tell a story.

One day she confided a little secret: "I was very well acquainted with Céleste Albaret, you know. We were friends. I met her when she was taking care of the Ravel house in Montfort-l'Amaury, where my nephew lives. She was a most refined and thoughtful person. She told me the most astonishing things about 'Mr. Proust,' as she called him."

Gisèle had been fascinated by Évelyne's anecdotes, stories that were recounted by an informant once removed, as it were. She had always come away fortified from a visit to the lady she called her adopted grandmother. And in

return she had brightened Évelyne's own life. When Évelyne died peacefully in her sleep, of a cardiac arrest that
had come quite without warning, Gisèle felt an immense
sadness, a feeling of immeasurable loss, of emptiness that
nothing could even begin to express. Except perhaps
for an obscure painting by Charles de Lafosse called *The
Sacrifice of Iphigenia* that contained a very dramatic representation of Timanthes' veil, and a few of Madame de
Sévigné's letters to her daughter. Gisèle was comforted somewhat when she inherited some of Évelyne's Chippendale
furniture, a Tiffany lamp in the form of a lush wisteria, a
Wedgwood tea service, and — Katicha. How could she have
guessed what had really been bequeathed to her, hidden
under the false bottom of the old rosewood secretary?

*

It was shortly after Évelyne's death that Gisèle had accepted Selim's eloquent invitation to a cup of tea. And
that invitation had been the start of another adventure, of
days and nights and months of waiting, of stolen moments, of fleeting hopes. Gisèle led the double life of a
mistress who waits in vain for the day her lover will leave
his legitimate wife. Statistics were not in her favor, but she
was confident, like all mistresses, that she would be the exception to the rule.

She was a changed woman. Yvonne was among the first
to notice: her eyes had an unaccustomed glow, her hair
a deeper luster, her repartee was more assured. Her colleagues at school started to call her the "autumn
bloomer." It was like a brief and intense blast of spring in
which everything had taken on a new set of colors, a new
set of flavors, a new life. Until the sordid breakup in the
café on the place Châtelet.

39

Gisèle hid her face in her hands in a vain effort to hold back this merciless tide of memories. She had to think of a plausible explanation to give the police for her comings and goings the day before, as close as possible to the truth without revealing anything important. There would be no disgrace in telling them that because of a bout of nervous depression, she had left her position at the school a year before and chosen to work for the Center for Distance Education in the solitude of her apartment. There would be no difficulty in explaining that Yvonne had met Adeline Bertrand-Verdon at a gala evening a few months later and had suggested that her sister, who was writing her thesis on Proust, might prove useful to her in some capacity or another. Gisèle could still remember every word of Yvonne's phone call that winter:

"Hi, Gise? Still correcting papers? You'll never guess who I met yesterday evening! A totally charming woman, the president of the Proust Association. She's looking desperately for an assistant. I told her about you. She's going to give you a call. Don't you think a change of pace would do you good? You haven't been looking well lately, always shut up indoors. Do make an effort and be nice to her, she knows everybody."

Adeline Bertrand-Verdon did in fact know just about everybody, and she was not disinclined to have as her secretary the sister-in-law of Jacques Thévenin, rheumatologist to the president of the Republic. So she put her best foot forward when she met Gisèle in the living room of her spacious apartment on the rue Saint-Anselme, where she served the tea herself, in a gesture that seemed almost homey.

"Your sister told me that you work on Proust's manuscripts," she began, sizing up Gisèle's navy blue suit with a rather condescending glance. She herself had on an elegant cashmere dress in shimmering hues, very fashionable that season.

"Yes, I'm writing a thesis on the transitions between —"

"My, how fascinating. And who is your doctoral adviser?"

"Professor Verdaillan."

"Oh, that darling Guillaume. He's a friend of mine!" she exclaimed with a slight sound of the throat, the meaning of which Gisèle would soon learn the hard way. "Well now, this is what I expect of a secretary. . . ."

What Adeline Bertrand-Verdon expected of a secretary explained why she had never been able to keep one for more than a month or two. But Gisèle was not privy to that piece of information when she agreed to become Adeline's "research assistant" — that is, her woman-in-waiting, her servant for everything, her slave, for a salary scarcely above minimum wage.

She would never have had the courage even to pay the president of the Proust Association a visit if she hadn't made an accidental discovery, just two weeks before Yvonne had called her, that roused her from the state of intellectual lethargy in which she had vegetated ever since Selim had left her. It was as though something had clicked: as though, watching over her, Évelyne had waited patiently for just the right moment to give her the signal — via Katicha.

For some time the cat had seemed rather listless. Her silvery gray fur had lost its luster, her yellow eyes were always half-closed, and she had all but stopped eating. She didn't even signal her desire to go out onto the little balcony — by means of a loud meow at the most unseemly hours — in order to munch a tiny leaf of the painstakingly maintained catnip that Gisèle had planted in a pot

41

for her exclusive use. In desperation Gisèle bought her some salmon, a dish she would normally have consumed with something approaching enthusiasm, but even the enticing pink slice of fish served on her favorite saucer failed to arouse her interest. It was time to call the vet.

The morning of the appointment, as though she had caught wind of something, Katicha disappeared. After looking for her under the bed, behind the curtains, in the laundry basket, and under the sofa, Gisèle lay down on the floor and looked in all directions until she finally caught sight of two glimmering, gilded crescents peering out from under the secretary.

"Come on, Katicha, be good now and come out of there," she said firmly. Katicha, clearly annoyed, flicked her tail and closed her eyes.

"I'm warning you, Katicha, if you don't come out of there immediately, I'm going to flush you out with — with the broomstick." Haughtily oblivious, her dainty chops drawn up in a kind of sarcastic sneer, Katicha turned a deaf ear on Gisèle's threats.

"Okay, you little monster, you asked for it," Gisèle called out. But she couldn't bring herself to use the broomstick, and she took up a slide rule instead and used it to poke about under the secretary. She didn't touch a hair of the cat, who was wedged between a leg of the desk and the wall. "Come on, Katicha, be sensible," she pleaded.

Just then the corner of the slide rule caught on a sort of protruding metal plate. Gisèle tried to pull it loose and tugged on it as hard as she could. In a cloud of gray dust, the double bottom of the desk gave way with a terrifying crash, spilling the contents of the desk's hidden compartment onto the wooden floor. Fifteen or twenty notebooks with black covers, filled with the inimitable scribblings of

Marcel Proust, tumbled into a heap right in front of the young woman's eyes. Dumbfounded, she turned her head to the side and found herself face to face with Katicha, who, after looking her up and down with a regal and triumphant gaze, sneezed three times and jumped up gracefully onto the sofa.

6

INSPECTOR FOUCHEROUX, standing with Gisèle in front of Aunt Léonie's house, suggested they find a place where they could talk without being disturbed. But first he had to take care of a few practical details.

"Have you decided what best to do about the symposium this afternoon?" he asked as gently as he could.

"Um, no . . . well, yes," Gisèle stammered, "but I don't know if . . ."

"You do understand that it can't take place here."

"Yes, I understand that. Perhaps it would be best if we canceled it altogether," she said flatly. "But with all these people who've come from so far away . . . and the minister . . ." The word stuck in her throat.

"The minister isn't coming," Foucheroux told her reassuringly. "I was at the mayor's house when the minister's office called with the change in plans. It's all for the better anyway, isn't it?"

"Yes, of course, but then Professor Verdaillan will still insist on giving his lecture, and it happens so rarely that

M. Brachet-Léger takes part in any sort of conference at all. . . . Perhaps," she went on, suddenly striking on an idea, "we could meet at the Marcel Proust Memorial High School. I know the principal."

"That's an excellent idea," Foucheroux said approvingly, "especially considering that no one will be allowed to leave the village until tomorrow anyway. And without a doubt, it's what Mme Bertrand-Verdon would have wanted."

"Probably," Gisèle agreed. "She would have wanted the show to go on. . . ."

"Why don't you go to the Old Mill Inn to set everything up, since that's where everybody is?" the inspector suggested.

Gisèle hesitated, then agreed, adding, "But it's two miles out of town, in the middle of the countryside. And I still don't have any money."

"In that case, allow me to help you out one more time by offering you half the rear seat of a local police car," he said, adding with a bitter smile, "I don't drive myself."

*

The Old Mill Inn, a large, square structure that was built in the eighteenth century, fully deserved its name. The walls were dotted with windows from one end to the other and draped in a web of Virginia creeper that made the building change color with the seasons. Pale green in the summer, red and gold in the fall, it had now reverted back to its veiny gray in preparation for the winter frost. A large wooden wheel protruded from its left side, turning to the rhythm of a brook that gurgled noisily below. Behind, one could just make out the banks of a tiny pond on which two immobile swans floated noiselessly. To the right, a

45

pergola overlooked the withered remains of a profusion of roses. A number of old stone benches, strategically positioned under an arbor, near the locks, and next to a footpath, tempted the observer to take a moment's rest in the garden, which was warmed by the sparkling rays of the winter sun.

The distressed owner, in a white chef's hat, met them at the door. "What a tragedy, what a tragedy!" he exclaimed by way of greeting. After a lengthy search they finally turned up a satisfactory suite for Inspector Foucheroux: a room on the ground floor that had an adjacent living room with a sufficient number of electrical outlets.

The owner's wife took her foul mood out on Gisèle. "Mlle Dambert already has a room," she snapped. "Number twenty-five, next to the room where Mme Bertrand-Verdon was staying, God rest her soul. But Mlle Dambert didn't pick up her keys yesterday evening."

Gisèle flushed. Inspector Foucheroux was well aware that she hadn't spent the night at the Old Mill Inn as she was supposed to, but it still seemed oddly as though she had misled him. For the first time he felt sorely the absence of his assistant. Nothing in this investigation was as it should be. It was all subterfuge, pretexts, illusions.

"I have a few phone calls to make," he said. "I'll meet you in twenty minutes. That'll give you time to get in touch with the high school."

It seemed to Gisèle that she had just received her marching orders. "Very good. In twenty minutes."

While she was walking toward the stairs, she heard the inspector inquiring about the comings and goings of Adeline and of Professor Verdaillan. She was sure that her name would come up next. She had twenty minutes to think up a satisfactory explanation. And to get hold of Émilienne, the unknowing keeper of the treasure.

As soon as he was alone in his room, Inspector Foucher-oux got right down to business and made three telephone calls that put him back on the track of standard procedure. He called his commanding officer, Charles Vauzelle, who was also his godfather, then Sergeant Tournadre, who had just got back from lunch. He had just hung up the telephone after talking with Detective Djemani when he heard a scarcely audible knock at the door.

"Come in, Mlle Dambert," he called out in a businesslike way, then asked her courteously to take a seat. He motioned toward one of the comfortable armchairs that furnished the little sitting room, which had a French window that opened onto a charming and sunny cobblestone terrace. "Since my assistant isn't here yet, I'll just take a few notes myself," he said as he opened a leather-bound notebook and took out a black fountain pen. Gisèle recognized the make. She had given one just like it to Selim!

She sat down on the edge of her seat like a bird ready to fly off at the least sign of danger. Not wanting him to see how nervous she was, she made a considerable effort to keep her hands crossed on her knees. Her blouse, with its white scalloped collar, made her look like a well-behaved little girl who had grown up a bit too fast.

"Your name is Gisèle Dambert. D-a-m-b-e-r-t." He spelled out her name. "And you were born in . . . ?"

"In a suburb of Tours."

So she was witty, too. Amused, he smiled for a second before rephrasing his question.

"And how old are you, Mlle Dambert? It is mademoiselle, isn't it?"

"Twenty-nine. And it's Gisèle. Gisèle Dambert." The battle had begun.

"How long had you been working for Mme Bertrand-Verdon?"

"Since last January. I was her research assistant," she answered, thinking, Nine months of hell.

He must have heard the tension in her voice, for when he went on his own voice was tinged with a measure of compassion. "And you preferred that to teaching?"

She chose her words carefully. "I left my position at the Claude-Bernard High School last year," she said evenly, "and took a position at the Center for Distance Education while working on my thesis, up until the time when I became Mme Bertrand-Verdon's assistant."

"I see," he said.

Gisèle stiffened. He saw only too well. He knew for a fact that the Center for Distance Education was a kind of asylum for teachers with problems, for the ones who suffered from depressions, who had nervous complexes, who were shy. He wondered what could have happened in Gisèle's life, what event had stamped the look of a hunted animal onto the blue eyes that peered out from beneath her long black lashes.

"How did you meet Mme Bertrand-Verdon?" he asked in as unthreatening a voice as he could muster, but he noticed that her lips tightened briefly at his question nevertheless.

"Through my sister, Yvonne Thévenin." She looked up to see if the name meant anything to him, but his stony gaze was impenetrable. He scribbled a few words on another page of his notebook.

"When did you last see Mme Bertrand-Verdon?"

"Yesterday." The word stuck in her throat.

"At what time?" he insisted.

"Around seven o'clock, at Aunt Léonie's. There were dozens of things that still had to be tended to before the

48

convention today. Which reminds me, I spoke to the principal. It's all set for the assembly hall at five o'clock."

"Perfect. So you didn't go to the dinner that was given here last night?"

"No, I . . . I had too much to do."

"Can you tell me who was there?"

"Oh, yes. I wrote out the invitations myself. There was Professor Verdaillan, Professor Rainsford, M. Desforge — of Martin-Dubois, the publishing house — and the Viscount of Chareilles. M. Brachet-Léger had informed us that he would not be arriving until today, at the last minute."

"I see. And there were no other women present?" Foucheroux asked on a sudden impulse.

"No," Gisèle answered, and hastened to explain: "Mme Verdaillan is unwell, Mme Rainsford stayed in America, M. Desforge has just been divorced. As for the Viscount of Chareilles —" She broke off discreetly. Foucheroux leaned toward her and gave her an encouraging look. She felt she had his undivided and well-meaning attention. This man must be a joy to talk to, normally, she thought.

"It's no secret, I suppose," she said out loud. "Mme Bertrand-Verdon was hoping to become the Viscountess of Chareilles and expected to announce her engagement at the convention."

"Was hoping?"

"That is to say —" Gisèle flustered. "It would be best if you spoke directly with —"

"I see your point," Foucheroux agreed. "We're almost finished. Do you know whether Mme Bertrand-Verdon had any enemies?"

Gisèle hesitated for a moment, but encouraged by the thought that the interview was almost over, she decided she would give frankness a try. "Mme Bertrand-Verdon did not have many friends. And she had no women friends at all. She hated other women."

"I am grateful to you for speaking so candidly," said Foucheroux. Then, mechanically rubbing his injured knee with his left hand, he looked her straight in the eyes and said, "One last thing. Where were you yesterday evening, during the hours between ten o'clock and midnight?"

"In my apartment in Paris, at thirty-five, rue des Plantes," she lied, looking off to one side and knowing perfectly well that he didn't believe a word of what she was saying.

7

PROFESSOR VERDAILLAN, who had received his Ph.D.
in literature from the University of Paris and had been
awarded the highest academic honors, had just finished a
succulent lunch in the soberly furnished dining room of
the Petit Roi restaurant in Chartres. Pike quenelles,
pheasant with red currants, chocolate charlotte, all served
with a knowledgeable selection of Bordeaux wines by a
highly competent and attentive staff.

He had good reason to grant himself a few hours of
respite, far from the crowd of Proustians who would
doubtless swarm around him before and after his lecture,
"Problematics of the Pluritext." He was rather pleased
with the title. Alleging the pressing need to verify a factual
detail in the Chartres Museum, he had eaten a quick
breakfast in his room at the Old Mill Inn, jumped into his
car, and driven at breakneck speed all the way to the famous cathedral so glowingly described by Péguy. After
taking a leisurely stroll through the streets of the old
town, stopping every now and then in a bookstore just

long enough to see which of his colleagues' books were not on display, he had arrived at the restaurant shortly before noon and lunched there alone and incognito. Taking advantage of the absence of his wife, who had been detained in Paris by the aftermath of a bad case of the flu, he had joyfully thumbed his nose at her repeated warnings about the insidious dangers of cholesterol and ordered just what he wanted. He was even thinking about allowing himself the luxury of a small glass of Armagnac after his second cup of coffee. After all, he was in excellent shape for a man of his age. True, he stooped a little, his hair was thinning out, and he needed to wear bifocals even when he wasn't reading. But all in all he was really quite fit, and he could still win an occasional tennis match, swim a long distance, and beat his children at Ping-Pong.

*

Guillaume Verdaillan was close to reaching the end of his career, a career as successful as it was traditional. He thought back to the years spent toiling away as a high school teacher, burdened by the extra hours he worked as an adjunct lecturer at the university trying to make his paycheck keep pace with the increasing demands of his growing family. What a lot of energy he had had in those days! But all of that was so long ago. He had been promoted to assistant professor after defending his thesis on Proust and, thanks in part to one of his schoolmates from college who came from a family less modest than his own, had netted a much-coveted associate professorship, from which he had needed to make just one more step up by obtaining the approval of a single committee in order to be named, finally, to a full chair. It had happened even faster than expected because of the suicide of one of his eminent colleagues at the University of Paris at Neuilly. The members of the search committee, unable to agree on a candidate — each faction pleading for someone from its own camp, the leftists for a Marxist, the others for a conservative — had finally been forced to give up and settle on a compromise. "All right, then — too bad! Verdaillan." And Verdaillan it was.

And so for several years now, Professor Verdaillan had been enjoying the relaxed life of a full professor, giving a few upper-level seminars, taking on an occasional master's thesis — the pages of which he used afterward to kindle the fire in the hearth of his country house in the Fontainebleau forest — and agreeing from time to time to direct a doctoral dissertation on the manuscripts of Marcel Proust, provided he would be able to put what his students had discovered to good use later on in his own research. He saw nothing dishonest in that, convinced as he was that only a mature mind like his own was capable of articulating the individual results of research in a coherent whole. In reality Guillaume Verdaillan was nursing a personal ambition, a project that he had set his heart on years earlier: to edit, by himself, a critical edition of Marcel Proust's complete works. He was categorically opposed to any kind of teamwork and had spoken derisively in public of the new editions, all of which were the questionable fruit of the uneven labors of a team of mostly foreign scholars. "No conception of the whole," he would thunder on the national public radio network. "A disaster of fragmentation," he said over and over at the symposiums that he attended dutifully in order to denounce the errors of his colleagues.

His publisher, Alphonse Martin-Dubois, Jr., had finally given up all hope of ever seeing the edition finished and long since shelved the project. Besides, he was not convinced that books by or on Proust were very profitable in the present climate. Proust was a classic, of course, but there was a lot of competition on the market, and it was perhaps a wise idea to let the thing die a natural death. The academics he sometimes had to deal with, alas, were known for their chronic fits of radical doubt, and there was a very good chance that the Verdaillan edition of Proust would never see the light of day. But miraculously, Guillaume Verdaillan had shown up in his office one day last June with an enormous manuscript under his arm, plunked the packet onto the table with a triumphant "Voilà!" and demanded that the whole thing appear in early November, to coincide with the lecture he was going to give at the convention of the Proust Association on the eighteenth. The lecture had been commissioned by the association's president herself, Mme Bertrand-Verdon. She had assured him that the minister of culture would attend and had promised him a surprise.

When Martin-Dubois objected to the time frame, Professor Verdaillan had gone crimson with anger. He threatened to annul his contract and bring suit, hinted that the Perpendicular Press was interested in the project, and added treacherously that he had already entered into negotiations with an American publisher for the sale of the translation rights. Weighing the financial pros and cons, and preferring not to make a mortal enemy of Verdaillan, who had a good deal of influence on the sale of textbooks, the publisher, caught off guard, called his associate to the rescue, hoping that Philippe Desforge would be able once again to find a good reason for putting things off until later. But to his great surprise, Desforge had shown an enormous enthusiasm for the idea, claiming that finding a printer near Paris in July and August would not be a problem, that the typesetter was not swamped with work, and that he would be able to supervise the proofreading himself. As for the publicity, he would take care of that as well. Alphonse Martin-Dubois stood open-mouthed at his associate's rash promises, but he assumed that Desforge had good reason to commit himself. He promised Guillaume Verdaillan that his edition would appear in November with his name on the cover and that he would receive a royalty of one and a half percent on the work's combined sales.

"In France and abroad," the professor insisted.

"In France and abroad," the publisher conceded and collapsed into a chair after glancing incredulously at Philippe Desforge. As soon as Guillaume Verdaillan had left, Martin-Dubois turned toward his associate and said, "I do hope you know what you're doing, old boy."

The associate publisher, dressed all in gray that after-noon, gave him a knowing smile and a reassuring "no problem" in response, then walked out the door.

No problem! It was an easy thing to say, but . . . Martin-Dubois ran a slender finger down his bony nose in a sign of impatience. Philippe had been acting quite bizarrely for some time. He dressed nicer than before, disappeared for long stretches of time without offering any explana-tions, worked at the oddest times of the day and night, and gave precedence to the strangest things, from a sur-prise voyage to Normandy to a fleetingly brief appearance on television. He was said to be going through a divorce, but he was more dynamic than ever. Younger, in a sense. Philippe Desforge was certainly no Don Juan. Everything about him was average: his unremarkable face, his stature, his talents, his ambitions. Doubtless this was what had made him such an excellent second man up until now. The publisher gazed skeptically at the hundreds of typed

55

pages piled up on the table in front of him. He could only hope that Philippe's editorial decisions had not been dictated by the urges of some midlife love affair. "If he loses me money, I'll put him out in a second," he said to himself. "And without Mathilde — if it's really true that they are getting a divorce — he'll be of virtually no use to me anyway."

*

Professor Verdaillan consulted his gold watch and discovered that he had let his postprandial reverie go on long enough. It was time to start back to Illiers if he still wanted to get in an hour or two of rest before his lecture. In a mood that had gone from good to better, he paid the bill, got back into his brand-new Renault, slipped a recording of *Athys* by the Arts Florissants into the cassette player, and allowed himself a moment of self-approbation. There had been quite a close call toward the end, but ultimately he had managed to turn things around and to regain the upper hand. That little snob of a Bertrand-Verdon was not going to put a spoke in *his* wheel. She did have friends in high places, true enough, and he had to admit that she had given him quite a fright, but nothing could happen to him now. He had discovered the perfect weapon to use in his defense. A satisfied smile took hold of his fleshy lips.

For a period of several months Adeline Bertrand-Verdon had quite literally courted him. She was constantly inviting him to evenings of chamber music, to cocktail parties with the members of the Proust Association, to "Proustian dinners." What she called her "Proustian dinners" were in fact nothing but an excuse to assemble around a table a group of people chosen for their relative usefulness in helping her to climb the social ladder, and who were more or less capable of appreciating the incomparable delicacy of a recipe that had been discovered in some crossed-out section of the manuscripts of Marcel Proust. At the last dinner, she had served young partridge and a mysterious dessert that she claimed to have found on the verso of a notebook that she refused to identify with any precision. That was not her custom. Generally, she liked to give an exact reference to the page of the manuscript from which the dish being served was taken. "This evening, we are eating from folio 54, recto, left margin, 1911," she would announce, in a parody of saying grace.

He knew perfectly well that she was not the one ruining her eyes deciphering the unpublished passages on gastronomy in the manuscripts of Marcel Proust at the Bibliothèque Nationale. She sent someone else to do it for her — most likely the young Dambert — and she . . . articulated everything in a coherent whole. But Adeline Bertrand-Verdon had her contacts at the Ministry of Culture and could function admirably as a go-between when it came time to organize a conference or to arrange for an invitation to go abroad. It was rumored that she knew Brachet-Léger personally and that she was an intimate friend of Philippe Desforge. Which is how she got Martin-Dubois Press to publish her *Guide of the Perfect Proustian*. The thing was utterly worthless. In fact it was nothing but an incongruous collection of sumptuous color photographs of so-called Proustian places — Paris, Cabourg, Illiers, Venice — with a chronology of the life of the author in the front and a slender bibliography in the back. In academic circles people made fun of it by referring to it spitefully as the *Guide of the Pseudo-Proustian* or *Everything*

You Always Wanted to Make People Think You Knew about Proust without Ever Having to Read Him. Nevertheless the book had sold rather well, due to a prodigious publicity campaign and to the fact that Adeline Bertrand-Verdon was undeniably a master of self-promotion.

He would never forget the rainy October day on which she had driven him to the wall. He realized now that she had sized up her chances of success and had waited for just the right moment to put the abominable deal on the table. She had invited him to lunch at her apartment and greeted him very warmly at the door. They had chatted about one thing and another until dessert, when, little by little, she had deftly brought him to mention his forthcoming edition of Proust's works. To his astonishment, she told him she knew all about it.

"And that reminds me," she went on, "I was wondering if you might be willing to postpone publication for a few months."

"Not on your life," he answered, sorely offended. "Things are already late as it is, and Alphonse Martin-Dubois himself promised me that the whole edition would appear next month."

"Oh, what a pity, what a terrible pity." She paused for a moment, then murmured as though she were talking only to herself, "So it won't be an edition of the complete works after all."

"What? But of course it will," he protested vehemently. "Everything that Proust ever wrote —"

"No, my dear friend, I'm afraid not. You're missing —" Her hazel eyes lit up with a derisive glow. "You're missing fifteen notebooks."

Guillaume Verdaillan thought for a second, then, suddenly reassured, retorted jovially, "Me and everybody else, if you're talking about the fifteen notebooks that were burned by Céleste Albaret at the behest of our great author. No one can make them rise from their ashes."

"And suppose for a moment that they were never burned, those notebooks? . . ." Adeline let her voice fall dramatically. "Suppose that a Proust scholar who was more adventurous than the others had discovered them, recently, in a private collection. . . ."

"You don't mean to say —" His voice died in his throat, and his heart started to throb uncontrollably. The 1905 manuscripts! The manuscripts that formed a bridge between Proust's first unfinished novel and his masterpiece! The manuscripts that would prove the existence of an earlier version of a key passage in *Remembrance of Things Past*, the originality of which was the cornerstone of his entire argument! The manuscripts that would destroy the hypotheses that he had built up so patiently and that were about to be published in just a few weeks! "It's not possible," he said out loud to reassure himself.

"Oh, but it is possible, you can believe me," said Adeline Bertrand-Verdon. "I have seen the notebooks myself." She leaned forward slightly and patted his hand as though to comfort him. She was shrouded in perfume, and the smell of the "most expensive scent in the world" penetrated his nostrils so suddenly that he felt sick to his stomach. He closed his eyes in a useless effort to block what was about to follow. But it did follow nevertheless. "I can understand what a terrible blow this discovery must be to you," she went on. "Not to mention what it does to the Martin-Dubois Press and to the whole Proustian community. But we still have some time left, and I'm sure we can find a way to work things out."

And she had gone on shamelessly to propose an "arrangement": she would give him access to the notebooks; he would postpone the publication of the complete works for a few months and would engage her as coeditor. Since her name began with a *B,* it would of course appear above his on the covers. Then, at the meeting of the Proust Association, he would announce the forthcoming publication of the *Complete Works of Marcel Proust,* — introduced, edited, and annotated by Adeline Bertrand-Verdon and Guillaume Verdaillan.

The blood drained from his face when he thought of all the diatribes he had made against editorial teamwork, establishing him as a scholar who always worked on his own. But at the same time, he knew how ridiculous he would look if Adeline published the notebooks elsewhere, invalidating his work and rendering his edition out-of-date almost as soon as it had rolled off the presses at Martin-Dubois.

She sat tranquilly observing him with a detached irony, judging perfectly the progression of thoughts and emotions taking hold of him. Like a deadly spider at the center of her web, gloating over her catch, she chose the propitious moment to cast the final thread that would tie him down for good: "You'll have to get used to the idea. Your publisher, by the way, will have no objections to the change. I spoke yesterday with Philippe Desforge — confidentially, of course. He's agreed. So there's no reason you can't give me your answer by tomorrow. And another thing. I've just heard that you'll be retiring in two years to begin what I'm sure will be an active and much deserved career as an emeritus. Your post at the university will be vacant. . . ." He looked at her in amazement. "I have some friends on the faculty there," she went on with a smile. "It will be the perfect position for me in two years. I'm sure that if you endorsed my candidacy . . ."

*

Guillaume Verdaillan tightened his grasp on the steering wheel. He could have strangled her in the moment she had spoken those words, and there was no way of knowing what might have happened if Gisèle Dambert hadn't shown up just then with an urgent message for Adeline. . . . He didn't like to think of the days of agony that had followed. He couldn't eat, couldn't drink. He could find no way out. He had felt like a laboratory rat trapped in a cage. Until the moment when, thanks indirectly to Max Brachet-Léger, he had found the perfect means of forcing her to back off. He savored the thought of his impending victory.

He turned in to the Old Mill Inn, going more than a little too fast, and barely missed colliding with a police car parked right in the middle of the courtyard. Grumbling about the abuse of authority and police privilege, he started up the stairs to his room. But what he heard just then made him freeze in midstride: "I still can't believe it! And she was such a good client, too. Murdered! Mme Bertrand-Verdon! I just can't believe it!"

*

At that very moment, in the magnificent living room of his villa on the impasse Montsouris in Paris, Max Brachet-Léger was in the throes of despair. He had been sitting beside the phone for hours, frozen, paralyzed by the thought that he had irretrievably lost the being dearest to him in all the world. He was huddled up in a black leather chair, his eyes half closed, his hair disheveled, in the midst of one of his famous fits of existential angst.

It had all started when Dominique had begged him to make an appearance at the convention of that Proust Association. He should have realized from the way

61

Dominique had insisted on it that something was amiss. In a moment of weakness — just the memory of which was enough to make him feel again that familiar state of inner commotion, pushing him to the threshold of retrospective ecstasy — he had said yes. But after the horrible fight they had had the day before, he had changed his mind. Dominique had walked out in the middle of the night, slamming the door on the way.

That morning, after hours spent at the window waiting vainly for Dominique to reappear, Max Brachet-Léger had decided to phone the association and cancel. It would be good for his image anyway. He tried to call Aunt Léonie's house. No answer. How ridiculous that there wasn't even a secretary in that pitiful association to take down a message! And all the while he was using the phone for such trifling matters, Dominique might call and get a busy signal! Exasperated, Max Brachet-Léger decided to send a telegram: "Impossible to come. Lost voice. MBL." That way, if Dominique was at the convention, he would be duly punished. If he was elsewhere . . .

The brilliant Parisian critic sank deeper into his chair, cradled his august head in his delicate hands, and like all the abandoned lovers in the world, he began to cry, his whole body shaking with great, pathetic, and uncomely sobs.

8

FROM THE WINDOW of his small but luxurious hotel room — exposed wooden beams, wall-to-wall carpet, private bath, television — Patrick Lester Rainsford, the American equivalent of Professor Verdaillan in a younger, more dashing, more dynamic version, had seen the police car drive up, and he was becoming increasingly nervous. For the second time he ran his hand absentmindedly through his thick, blond, carefully groomed hair. He tried to sustain a discreet resemblance to Hemingway, an appearance to which a number of his female students were less than indifferent, and he affected an Oxford accent on the pretext that his mother was English. He attributed his choice of academic discipline and his excellent pronunciation of French to the influence of a distant ancestor from Louisiana — but always failed to mention that she had probably emigrated with one of the shipments of prostitutes sent to New Orleans in the eighteenth century.

He had come to fulfill a mission. Not that he was a Proustian, heaven forbid! The ludicrous, old-fashioned idea of devoting his life to an author was anathema to him. No, what interested him was critical theory. He had published ten years previously a slender volume by way of a doctoral thesis that bore the ingenious title *Critique of the Critique of the New Criticisms: A Transatlantic View.* Very few people had understood a word of the book, but it contained a postface by his doctoral advisor, who not only called all the shots at his university's scholarly press but also had a very efficient means of putting pressure on one of the editors of the *New York Times Book Review.* This little volume — and the special protection it received from its author's formidable mentor — had rapidly elevated him to the rank of full professor at a university of his choice. From the day of his arrival he had made a point of participating with great enthusiasm and panache at numerous committee meetings. He was soon moving in the fashionable circles of the local elite, who were charmed by his British accent, and he had chosen, at the propitious moment, a wealthy young bride who made no demands on him at all and worshiped his every move. When it came time to choose a new chairman for the department of Romance languages, it was only natural that his name be put at the top of the list. It wasn't long before he had systematically built up a sizable following and a solid reputation. For the last several months he had assiduously attended services at the Episcopalian Church, thinking it would help his chances of being appointed university dean. Everything was practically in the bag. One last hurdle remained for him to take, which is why he had come to the convention of the Proust Association.

He had already violated college tradition in a sacrilegious but profitable way by introducing the didacto-interactive computer method of second-language acquisition into the lower-level language courses — an innovation that had led to skyrocketing enrollments in French — and he had hired (and fired, when the need arose, in accordance with the rapidly changing fashions in literary criticism) a structuralist, a Marxist, a deconstructionist, and a feminist. He had just recruited a specialist in francophone literature and postcolonial studies. And now he needed desperately to find a renowned geneticist for his Center for Postmodern Manuscripts. And to be elected to the Legion of Honor. After that he could watch everyone else battle it out among themselves from the height of his new position. When he had heard that the minister of culture would honor the autumnal convention of the Proust Association with his presence and that the famous critic Brachet-Léger, whom scarcely anyone had ever seen, let alone spoken to, would also deign to say a few words, he had immediately jumped at the opportunity and into the first plane (Air France, since the food there was not quite as bad, and he prided himself on his discriminating taste) from Boston to Paris. Everything would have gone "as smooth as butter," as France's younger generation would put it nowadays, if it hadn't been for Adeline Bertrand-Verdon.

On his arrival in Paris a few days earlier, Patrick Rainsford had thought nothing unusual about the message left for him at his hotel inviting him to a tea with the president of the Proust Association. He hadn't responded immediately, of course, so as not to be tied down if something more interesting turned up — an evening at the Ministry of Culture, a government-financed dinner at the Ritz, the opening of some exhibition or other where it would be good for him to be seen. On the other hand, the minister himself — or his wife — might make a brief appearance at Bertrand-Verdon's tea, and if Jerry Lewis, Kirk Douglas, and a multitude of other Americans had all been decorated recently by the French government, why not prepare the way for his own nomination to the Legion of Honor or, at the very least, for his Palmes Académiques, the medal given for excellence in the service of education in France? Of course he could scarcely hope to find Brachet-Léger at such a function, but thinking that he could always use the insidious effects of jet lag as an excuse to cancel at the last minute, he had finally decided to accept. The secretary assured him on the phone that "Mme Bertrand-Verdon would be delighted to see him." She had a nice voice, the secretary did.

"Potentially attractive brunette, if she would only go to the trouble to dress properly," he thought when Gisèle greeted him at the door in a pretentious building on the rue Saint-Anselme. The apartment, with white plaster walls and fake Fortuny drapes, was cluttered with a studied mix of Victorian furniture and all manner of books that attested to the inhabitant's eclectic tastes in things literary, or at least to her desire to show that she did in fact read books. Just as he entered the living room, the members of a quartet were taking their seats. Just his luck! He hated chamber music. But it was too late to retrace his steps. Adeline Bertrand-Verdon had seen him.

"Ah, here's Professor Rainsford," she sang out. "This way, my friend, this way . . . We would never have started without you. . . ."

He had met her once at the embassy in Washington — or was it in New York? — where she had provoked in him the same feeling of bemused repulsion. Adeline Bertrand-Verdon knew how to dress. The fashionably cut black gown she was wearing was set off by a heavy braided-gold necklace with earrings and bracelets to match. And she knew, indisputably, how to make herself up. The pale green eye shadow was just the nuance needed to give depth to what were in fact quite ordinary brown eyes and to emphasize her thick fringe of black hair, which had been dyed and trimmed to perfection. The rouge, on her rather overly elevated cheekbones, was applied strategically to distract attention from her lips, which, too thin, had been deftly painted to appear thicker than they really were, and from her chin, which was too pointed but could have seemed attractively chiseled when seen from a distance.

Why, then, did Patrick Rainsford feel the almost uncontrollable urge to shy away from this face smiling up at him so amiably, to recoil from this diamond-laden hand stretched out so amicably toward his? She's a phony, he thought instinctively, to which a second voice in him replied, Birds of a feather . . . Out loud he said, "What a pleasure it is to see you again, Adeline. The last time we met, it was on the other side of the ocean, if I remember correctly. . . ."

He took the hand held out to him and was introduced to a small number of people whose useless names he made a point of forgetting immediately, with the exception of Philippe Desforge, who was still somewhat influential at Martin-Dubois Press, and Viscount Edward of Chareilles, who might invite him at some point to stay at one of his châteaux. Verdaillan was there, of course, with whom he talked shop for a few moments while letting his gray-blue eyes wander casually from one member of the little group to the next. It was hard to believe there wasn't a woman in the room that he could put in his "F" (for "fuckable") category. Except, perhaps, for the secretary. Clearly neither the minister, nor his wife, nor Brachet-Léger was expected. The musical part of the afternoon was even more boring than he had feared. But the sandwiches afterward were catered by Fauchon, the different brews of tea were more than palatable, and the champagne was of an honorable vintage. . . .

He was just getting ready to leave with the first batch of guests when Adeline Bertrand-Verdon turned on her heels and stood facing him, blocking his path to the door. "My dear Patrick, don't disappoint me by running off so quickly. Stay just another moment," she said, putting a surprisingly firm hand on his left arm. "Do wait just a minute," she whispered in a playfully conspiratorial tone, "while I get rid of all these people as fast as I can." The professor was very annoyed. He knew all about the whimsies of French women, but surely she wasn't crazy enough to —

She had a hard time getting rid of the viscount, but with a cozily persuasive "Come, come, my dear friend, we *are* seeing each other later on, you know," and some prodigious fluttering of the eyelids, she managed to get him out the door. Patrick Rainsford was getting more and more confused. If she was going to meet the viscount later, why on earth had she virtually commanded him to stay?

She must want me to invite her to the university to give a lecture, he thought. But with the two or three little articles she got published in those obscure journals on the strength of her connections, and with her ridiculous *Guide of the Perfect Proustian*, I simply cannot, cannot ask her to come.

"Well, there we are, finally, just the two of us," she said with a smile that revealed her wolfish teeth.

"Indeed," he said prudently, rather ill at ease.

"Let's make ourselves comfortable," she suggested, gesturing toward a gilded settee. "You must be wondering why I am imposing on you this way." She cast her eyes down modestly.

"I do have a dinner invitation to go to," he lied without batting an eye.

"Oh dear, I should have known as much," she murmured wryly, and added out loud, "I'll get right to the point, then. I understand that you are founding a center for manuscript studies. . . ."

He was genuinely surprised that she had heard about it. The plan for the project was known only to three or four university administrators and a couple of colleagues he had not waited to tell because he couldn't resist another chance to make them feel jealous. At a time when everyone was making drastic budget cuts, he had been given thousands of dollars and a free hand to found his own center of genetic studies. They had all been bowled over by his vision of a curriculum for the twenty-first century. The Franco-American world was definitely a small one, too small to avoid such leaks. Either that or he was too famous. This last idea was a comfort to him.

"I am in fact thinking of establishing a center that would acquire modern as well as postmodern manuscripts, a kind of laboratory for the analysis of present-day writing," he launched off before he could stop himself. "But not in the immediate future," he hastened to add. "You simply cannot imagine the amount of work involved in getting such a project off the ground."

"I can imagine it all too well. I am sometimes overwhelmed by the administration of the Proust Association, which is on a much smaller scale. You will be needing, then, someone who can coordinate matters on a day-to-day basis. You can't do six different things at once," she said emphatically.

He saw now what she was getting at and judged that it was time to bring the little conversation to a close. There were several ways of going about it. He decided to evade the issue as shrewdly as possible. "You're certainly right about that, Adeline. And I'm looking. The only prerequisite, since the center will be financed by private American foundations, is that the person I appoint be an American citizen."

"Oh, well," she said, "there must be dozens of ways to get around that." And, when she saw that he was about to get up and object, she added, widening a malicious smile that contrasted sharply with the evil gleam in her green eyes: "Before we go on, I must tell you, Patrick, that I was at a cocktail party last summer where, purely by chance, I met Laura Peterson's sister."

He didn't move a muscle, but his sudden pallor must have given him away, since she said immediately, in a tone of ironic concern: "A little bourbon, Patrick? Or cognac?" He shook his head, and she went on mercilessly: "As I was saying, you're going to need an assistant who is familiar with the current trends in genetic criticism. Don't you think the convention of the Proust Association would be the right moment to announce your choice? We're talking about next September, of course. I won't be . . . available until then."

"It's not just up to me, I'm afraid," he tried one last time to object.

"Oh, but my dear friend, everyone knows that you do precisely as you please. With your reputation. Which you certainly wouldn't want to lose, would you, now? And you would lose it, Patrick, if it ever came out who really wrote your *Critique of the Critiques of the New Criticisms.* . . . But no one needs to know about it. Laura's letters aren't in the public domain, thank God. It's a little less than fifty years ago now that she . . . disappeared, shall I say? and —" A little noise over by the door, which was standing slightly ajar, caused her to break off suddenly.

"Gisèle!" she almost screamed.

The young woman's slender silhouette, with its long, flowing hair, appeared in the doorway. It seemed to Patrick Rainsford that the angel of mercy typical of Pre-Raphaelite paintings had appeared before him.

"What on earth, Gisèle, you're still here? I thought you had left . . . a long time ago. . . ."

"But, madame, you told me to finish typing the labels —"

"So you were in my office," Adeline Bertrand-Verdon said accusingly.

"Well yes, madame, you asked me to," Gisèle protested clumsily. "I've finished. I was about to go home."

"Fine, Gisèle, do just that. And be here tomorrow at ten o'clock sharp," she said in the exasperated tone of a mistress who is always having to remind her servants of their duties. Taking advantage of the situation, Patrick Rainsford got up. "I have to leave as well."

"Oh yes, your . . . dinner," said Adeline Bertrand-Verdon, turning her somber gaze back in his direction. "Go ahead then, since we're agreed. We are agreed, aren't we?"

"I'll give you a call," he said by way of good-bye.

"Fine, give me a call. At any rate, we'll see each other at the Old Mill the evening before the convention. We can work out the details after dinner. Gisèle will call you a cab, if you like. . . ."

*

71

"The bitch," he said to himself furiously, "the bitch!"

He really had seen her again, at last night's dinner. Every dish had been torture, from the asparagus to the chicken in sauce financière to the strawberries in cream. And he had seen her afterward, in Aunt Léonie's house, stretched out on the floor in her checked suit, pitiful and finally silent, her right temple split open by the blood-stained feet of a statue.

9

BY FOUR O'CLOCK IN THE AFTERNOON the crowd in the Original Madeleine bakery was overflowing onto the sidewalk of the village square. The daylight had faded, and the last rays of the sun had transformed the little gray plaza into a poetic site, casting a reddish yellow glow onto the picturesque old houses that faced the church, which with their exposed wooden beams and diamond-shaped windows had a vaguely Dutch air about them. The square reverberated with the sounds of numerous foreign tongues.

The wildest rumors were making the rounds in a variety of more or less accurate translations, and the news that the president of the Proust Association had been murdered had taken on an international importance that would not have displeased the president herself had she still been alive.

Those who had gone directly to Aunt Léonie's had found two imperturbable policemen guarding the door and a handwritten sign whose shakily formed letters informed them that "For reasons beyond our control, the convention of the Proust Association will take place in the auditorium of the Marcel Proust Memorial High School." It had been tacked to the door by the association's volunteer guide, André Larivière, an aging retired tax inspector who was an avid reader and a guardian of tradition. He was objecting vociferously to the presence of a film crew that had chosen this particular day to do their location shots. "Aunt Léonie's house is not a circus ring!" he shouted, his voice quavering with indignation. "It was the site of an historic event, and I insist that you respect the memory —"

"But I've told you three times already," a fair-haired young man screamed back at him, his face crimson with anger. "We have authorization from the president herself. I've got her letter right here." He held up an envelope that did in fact bear the seal of the Proust Association. "We got here late because of all the farmers' demonstrations on the roads."

"Johnny, Johnny, take it easy," said an older, rather dandyish man who walked up with two cameramen, a makeup artist, and a photographer at his heels. "I'm Ray Taylor," he added with a dazzling smile, as if the revelation of his identity would solve everything.

"André Larivière," the elderly gentleman responded militarily, straightening his bow tie. "I don't know what more I can do to impress upon you and your . . . team that you should take your operation to the Marcel Proust Memorial High School. That's where the events are to take place."

After venting his ill humor in language that bordered on the obscene, Ray Taylor complied, leaving the volunteer guide standing guard in front of the house like a victorious watchdog. Out of the corner of his eye, the old man caught sight of Émilienne at the end of the street, and he waved her over frantically. "Émilienne," he said, puffing like a bellows, "if we want to avoid another catastrophe, we're going to have to join forces. Can you take my place here and point the new arrivals toward the high school? I ran into M. Desforge, who was dumbfounded by the news, as you can imagine, but I'm not sure if the Viscount of Chareilles has been informed —"

"And what about Mlle Dambert?" Émilienne asked. "She gave me her bag to look after, and it's not exactly light, I can tell you that."

"Give it to me. She called me from the Old Mill. She's the one, poor girl, who's going to stand in for the president at the opening of the convention —"

"But I left it at the Café de la Gare," Émilienne admitted recalcitrantly, anticipating what he was about to say. "I wasn't going to lug it around all day without knowing when I would see her again —"

"I haven't got time to go by the Café de la Gare. I absolutely must get to the high school to keep them posted on the latest developments."

"What latest developments?"

"Oh! I forgot you haven't heard yet. We've just received a telegram from M. Brachet-Léger. He can't come. He's lost his voice!"

"Or so he says," Émilienne grumbled. That was simply not done in her world, canceling like that at the last second. But André Larivière had already turned on his heels and was making his way toward the school as fast as his eighty-year-old legs would carry him to announce the bad news.

*

75

At the Old Mill Inn, after he had let Gisèle Dambert go tend to her affairs, Inspector Foucheroux had left two messages, one for Patrick Rainsford, the other for Guillaume Verdaillan, summoning them to speak with him immediately after the convention. Then he had asked to see the room that Adeline Bertrand-Verdon had been staying in, knowing that Sergeant Tournadre had left instructions for the hotel staff to leave everything untouched.

He was shown to a charming room with flowered wallpaper and rustic furniture arranged with the somewhat sterile tidiness of hotel rooms, in spite of two surprising original engravings depicting scenes from the *Golden Legend*. He noticed that the bed had not been slept in and that a rose had been laid on the pillow next to a chocolate in a silver wrapper. On the old-fashioned nightstand there was a bottle of mineral water, a crystal glass, a spoon, and a small pot of jam — rose-petal jam, according to the label. On the little desk between the two windows there was a lamp, a small sheaf of stationery with the letterhead of the Old Mill Inn, and a black kid-leather purse, lying ajar on its side. Taking care not to disturb any fingerprints that might be recovered later, Foucheroux examined the contents of the purse and found exactly what he expected: a soft leather wallet with a compartment for paper money and another for credit cards that also contained a pink driver's license in the name of Adeline Bertrand, née Verdon, born forty years earlier in Nemours and residing on the rue Saint-Anselme in Paris. The little color photograph was attractive enough, but the arrogant smile tugging at the woman's red-painted lips lent a mocking, cold air to her triangular face. In another pouch of the purse there was a makeup kit with lipstick, foundation, mascara, and eye shadow, as well as a gold pen with the initials *ABV* engraved on the cap, a pad of high-quality stationery, and an address book riddled with corrections. Everything that belonged in the purse of a perfect businesswoman, except for a calendar and a set of keys.

Foucheroux surmised that Adeline Bertrand-Verdon must have left her room in a such a rush that she hadn't even taken the bare minimum, not even her purse or her coat. A glance into the wardrobe, where he found a stunning silver-fox pelisse hanging next to two designer gowns and a red wool suit, confirmed his supposition. The only thing she had taken with her were her keys. He would have given the world to know what had brought the president of the Proust Association to leave this snug refuge so precipitously for the lifeless chill of Aunt Léonie's house at such a late hour of the evening. According to the owners of the hotel, Adeline Bertrand-Verdon had indicated she was retiring for the night and asked not to be disturbed when she went to her room.

In a little suitcase lying open on the dresser across from the bed was a Hermès scarf, some spare lingerie, a white lace nightgown with a bathrobe to match, two velvet slippers, and a pair of high-heeled boots. The drawers of the dresser had not been used. To the left, the door to the impeccably clean green-and-white-tiled bathroom stood ajar. Inside, a rumpled towel and an enormous toilet bag were the only visible signs of the occupant's brief passage. Beyond the usual toiletries, Jean-Pierre Foucheroux noticed several different kinds of pharmaceutical products: aspirin, antidepressants, sleeping pills, vitamins, and an analgesic ointment.

"A regular pharmacy," he said to himself as he sat down on the Voltaire chair that had been reupholstered to match the bedspread and the curtains. A perfect room for a woman who liked to coordinate her colors all the way down to her underwear, he caught himself thinking. He became aware almost suddenly of the peculiar texture of the silence in the room. It reminded him of a plushly padded box. Trusting his intuition, he let his gaze wander about from object to object. Often he had found that, independently of the routine tasks of an investigation, if he could manage to relax completely, he would notice a detail that would reveal much more to him than he would have learned by trying to force the places, the facts, and sometimes the people to talk. Once some yoga exercises that he had learned in his youth had gotten him out of a hopeless situation. Along with the help of Leila Djemani. His eyes lit on a pot of jam that had clearly been opened and on the rather dull little silver spoon lying next to it. He knew immediately just what to do. To make sure, he called the hotel operator, who connected him with the kitchen. He was told that the breakfast menu included honey, strawberry jam, raspberry jam, and sometimes bitter orange marmalade, but the Old Mill Inn did not stock rose-petal jam, an exotic product little suited to the rustic style that had given the inn its distinctive reputation.

The next step, after sending the pot of jam off to the laboratory, was to go to the convention of the Proust Association to observe the participants. A pity only that Leila wouldn't be there with him. Her extraordinary intuition — he would have said "women's intuition" in his more sexist days — made her a most valuable colleague. He smiled at the memory of how furious he had been when Charles Vauzelle had quite literally forced her upon him three years earlier. And of that first stony meeting, fraught with mutual mistrust and resentment. For he was no more inclined to collaborate with this tall, badly dressed, brown-haired, and rather portly woman than was she to be put at the disposition of Vauzelle's favorite, who had just been handicapped in an automobile accident that had killed his pregnant wife. Having nothing in common, they got off to a rough start. Now they had become a team whose numerous successes in clearing up the most difficult cases had made them into something of a legend. They were given an unheard-of degree of freedom to intervene in criminal investigations to which they were not technically assigned. They were even able to laugh together at the nicknames people gave them behind their backs: Chipmunk and Gimpy.

*

The corridors of the high school were an absolute chaos. Mischievous students had taken down the cardboard arrows indicating the way to the assembly hall and put them back up so that they pointed in all the wrong directions, and anyone who didn't know the building was likely to wander for some time from floor to floor. Fortunately, André Larivière knew where he was going. He found Gisèle Dambert standing together with Philippe Desforge and Professor Verdaillan in the entry hall in front of the auditorium, battling it out with Ray Taylor's film crew. He pushed his way through to the secretary and, without saying a word, handed her Max Brachet-Léger's telegram. "Oh, no!" she exclaimed before she could stop herself.

"What's happened now?" asked Guillaume Verdaillan impatiently.

"M. Brachet-Léger won't be joining us. An acute case of laryngitis —"

"Say, that's a new one. Usually he has the flu," joked the professor. "It's no big problem, anyway. It'll give me more time for my lecture."

"A number of people are going to be very disappointed," Philippe Desforge said underhandedly. "At any rate, as a member of the board of directors, I believe the important thing now is that the convention take place, whatever the circumstances, and I would be most grateful to you, Mlle Dambert, if you would give the opening remarks. My own emotional involvement prevents me from speaking, but may I recommend to you the following approach —"

He took Gisèle by the arm and led her into a corner while Guillaume Verdaillan spouted off in front of Ray Taylor's camera team. Since he could not get into the Aunt Léonie's house to make his documentary, the British producer thought he might as well take advantage of the convention and start in on a made-for-TV movie about the murder of the Proust Association's late president. Catching sight of Gisèle talking with Philippe Desforge in the corner, he struck on a brilliant idea. He walked to where she was standing, sized her up, wrinkled his nose, and nodded discreetly in the direction of his makeup man.

"Can you fix her up?"

"Sure. Give me half an hour, a scarf, earrings, and a pair of high-heeled shoes."

"Got it," said the producer as he walked straight up to his new Cinderella with a big smile on his lips, waving his hands about like a modern-day sorcerer.

*

In the assembly hall, sitting in the glow of a glorious sunset that was flooding in through the room's cathedral windows, Inspector Foucheroux made out several different groups among the fifty or so people present. In the first row there were the elite of the village, among whom he recognized the mayor, locked in conversation with an elderly, monocled gentleman wearing a medal on his lapel and a signet ring on his left hand. Just behind them were a few intellectuals from a variety of academic factions, students and professors with pen and paper at the ready, a good number of foreigners conversing in English, and at the back, a number of lone wolves spread out among the remaining empty seats.

At ten past five, just as people were beginning to get fidgety, a young woman with her hair done up in a kind of bronze-colored halo around an oval face, the shape of which had been accentuated by some rather outlandish blue-glazed earrings, stepped up to the microphone affixed to the lectern, focused on the crowd, and began to speak. Very few of those present recognized Gisèle Dambert, who had been transformed by an enormous silk scarf and a pair of fashionable Italian pumps into a vision of self-confidence, an image that could not have been further from her true state of mind. While two prodigious cameras stared at her with their implacable eyes, she started to deliver the little speech that had been more or less foisted upon her, speaking at first in a noticeably shaky voice.

"Ladies and gentlemen, honored members and guests of the Proust Association, it is my most unfortunate task to have to inform you this afternoon of the violent death, yesterday evening, of our president. . . ." Foucheroux shifted suddenly on his chair, which creaked loudly. "As Mme Bertrand-Verdon would most certainly have wanted the convention she herself organized to take place regardless of the circumstances," Gisèle went on, "it has been decided that the symposium will go on as planned, with one slight modification, beyond the room change, for which we must again beg your indulgence. We would like to extend our thanks to the principal of the Marcel Proust Memorial High School for his generous help. I regret,

81

however, to inform you that M. Max Brachet-Léger has taken ill and will not be joining us today. . . ." A moan of disappointment rolled through the hall, and someone barked out a vulgar word. "But Professor Verdaillan will give his lecture," Gisèle pursued, "and the police have assured us that M. André Larivière will be allowed to take us on a partial tour of Aunt Léonie's house tomorrow afternoon at two o'clock. We hope therefore that in spite of the tragic events weighing on this day, your presence at this symposium will allow us to commemorate the death of Marcel Proust and to give his work a new life through a new interpretation of the texts that —" A concerted burst of loud applause from an unidentified source cut Gisèle Dambert off in midsentence, and she blushed in embarrassment. "Professor Verdaillan of the University of Paris at Neuilly," she announced by way of conclusion, waving pathetically toward the front right corner of the hall.

Fully sure of himself, Guillaume Verdaillan stood up, extracted a sheaf of papers from his briefcase, adjusted the sit of his glasses, and with a brief "Thank you, Gisèle" launched into his lecture, taking care only to replace the customary "It is a great pleasure" with a more suitable "It is a sad honor to speak to you today of the problematic of the pluritext. . . ."

He went on for an hour and forty minutes, despite signs of growing fatigue on the part of his listeners, most of whom considered it a feat they had no intention of repeating to have given *Remembrance of Things Past* a single reading from cover to cover. As soon as Professor Verdaillan had finished, a little pale man appeared out of nowhere, grabbed the microphone with a leather-clad hand, thanked the professor in the name of the board of directors, announced that because of the late hour, he would not ask the lecturer to entertain questions, and pronounced the convention closed, to the great relief of everybody present except one.

Foucheroux turned toward Sergeant Tournadre, who had entered the hall discreetly and sat down at his side. In response to the inspector's questioning gaze, he whispered in his hear: "Philippe Desforge. And next to him, with the monocle, the Viscount of Chareilles."

10

IN THE HUBBUB THAT FOLLOWED, Foucheroux couldn't hear much of what was being said around the room, but as he made his way toward the lecturer he caught a snatch of what Philippe Desforge was saying to the gentleman with the monocle: "— and as a result, I don't see why you would be nervous, since you were at the Château de la Moisanderie." Taking advantage of the situation, Foucheroux politely introduced himself to the two men, whose stature, demeanor, and facial expression formed a striking contrast.

"Inspector Foucheroux, of the Criminal Investigation Department. M. Desforge," he said to the shorter of the two, "may I speak to you for a moment?"

"Now?" said the associate publisher indignantly, projecting the image of a terribly busy man.

"The sooner the better," the inspector replied quietly, without losing any of his natural authority.

"Well, look, if it really can't wait, let's say . . . uh . . . in an hour or two. There are still some things I have to do for the association, and I'll have to make sure the cocktail party has been canceled at the Old Mill —"

"Shall we say nine o'clock, then, in room five?" the inspector said politely.

Philippe Desforge hesitated for a moment before muttering a recalcitrant "Very well." While they were talking, the other gentleman had been standing perfectly still, visibly indifferent, his disdainful gaze directed away from the milling crowd. Foucheroux tried a direct approach.

"Viscount —"

"Chareilles. Edward of Chareilles, Viscount of Omboy," he stated dryly.

"You are also one of the members of the board —"

"Correct." He drew out the r's in the word in a way that bordered on insolence.

"— and you were a personal friend of the president," Foucheroux went on without losing a beat. His godmother was a marquise.

Just then a lady in a navy blue coat, her hair done up in an elegant chignon, interrupted them. "Edward, my dear, we're leaving," she announced with an enunciation that revealed either high birth, an elite education, or speech lessons.

"Straightaway, Marie-Hélène." He paused for an instant. "I am expected elsewhere, Inspector. If you would excuse me —"

"But of course," said Foucheroux without the least hesitation, but added in a more official tone, "Where can I reach you tomorrow morning?"

"Oh! Well, at the Moisanderie, I would think." And with that rather offhand remark, he rushed off as though he were trying to keep his distance from some disgusting parasite. Foucheroux couldn't resist an indulgent smile. He knew the type.

85

Gisèle Dambert had taken refuge in the little room adjoining the assembly hall and was trying to figure out how to extract herself, once and for all, from Professor Rainsford's courtly glances and Ray Taylor's bits of advice. From the moment André Larivière had told her that Émilienne had left the bag she was keeping for her at the Café de la Gare, she had had but one thing on her mind: to get it back. She realized now how careless she had been, but she hadn't worried about it then because the bag was locked and she had the key. She was getting more nervous by the second, and she was intent on slipping off as soon as possible — but without appearing too anxious to get away. No one must suspect what was hidden inside that bag.

*

Bernard Tournadre suggested to Jean-Pierre Foucheroux that they eat dinner together, but the inspector declined; he had to question two possible witnesses that evening at the Old Mill and wait for his assistant to arrive.

"Let me at least drive you over."

"That's very kind of you, but if you don't mind, I would prefer to keep the driver that you already assigned me. But before I go, there's something I'd like to ask Gisèle Dambert."

"Aha! 'Where were you on the evening of,' I suppose?"

Foucheroux had to give the sergeant credit for his perspicacity. "That's right," he acknowledged. "How many people, in your opinion, know that it was last night Mme Bertrand-Verdon was killed?"

"Besides us and the murderer? Oh, well, it's hard to keep a secret around here. It's a small town —"

"Nevertheless, I think it's a tack we should pursue."

Tournadre gave him a puzzled look. "She's an odd person, Mlle Dambert," he conceded. "Rather serious and reserved. Émilienne, the housekeeper who found the body, didn't like her at first. She thought her —"

Just then, they saw Gisèle Dambert trying to work her way discreetly toward the exit, but her height and her elaborate hairdo caught everyone's attention. She was stopped first by Philippe Desforge, who spoke to her with evident urgency, then, just as she had agreed to what he wanted, by Professor Verdaillan.

"So, Mlle Dambert," the professor inquired in a booming voice, "just how far along are you with that thesis of yours?"

Out of kindness, Foucheroux hastened over to the little group to help Gisèle out of an awkward position. But to his astonishment, she cringed when he asked to speak to her alone for a moment.

"I'm sorry, I'm not done yet," she said frigidly. "Can we put it off until later? . . ."

Foucheroux observed her intently. Beneath her makeup she was quite pale, and she was making an enormous effort to control her emotions. Gisèle Dambert was on the verge of a nervous breakdown. He decided not to press her any further, not to take advantage of the weakness he could see in her cloudy eyes and trembling bare hands. "Why don't we meet tomorrow morning?" he said comfortingly. "You'll be at the Old Mill, won't you? Shall we say eight o'clock, if that's not too early?"

"Eight o'clock," she repeated, visibly relieved to have escaped the ordeal of an on-the-spot interrogation. She turned to Professor Verdaillan, who hadn't missed a syllable of the exchange. "Could I meet with you at some point?"

"Of course . . . Come see me when you're done with the inspector," he said cavalierly. Gisèle nodded and walked straight to the exit, oblivious to the murmurs and the questioning glances she left behind her. Only when she got outside did she feel as though she could breathe again. It was dark now, and much cooler. Cars were parked on the sidewalk all the way up to the church. Gisèle took the shortest path, oblivious to the warm glow emanating from the windows of the low houses she passed, inside which daily life was going on tranquilly as usual.

Built in a series of concentric circles around the church, the entire village was wedged in between the railroad tracks and the river, each house holding up its neighbor for as long as anyone could remember. The medieval ruins in the middle were surrounded by a circle of less ancient constructions, themselves enclosed in the ring of modern buildings that constituted the new part of town. Gisèle took a street that cut straight through the various rings. Bits of text were echoing in her mind — *like enormous incisions that divide the village so neatly in four that it resembles a cross bun, the sections of which still adhere but have already been separated . . .* She avoided the avenue de la Gare and walked to the rear entrance of the café, too preoccupied to notice the shadow that had been following her silently all the way from the high school, matching his footsteps to hers, and who slipped into the doorway of an empty house as Gisèle walked into the "Hôtel de Guermantes."

In reality this was nothing but a small-town café with red-and-white-checked curtains, a bar, and an adjoining dining room that had originally been part of a private apartment. The menu was rather unremarkable, but the ingredients were all of good quality and the prices more than reasonable. Gisèle, however, was in no mood to eat. She went straight to the bar, where a number of local patrons were having a drink before dinner, and asked the waitress timidly if she could have the bag that Émilienne had left for her that morning. The young redhead gave Gisèle a less than kindly look. She didn't like Parisian women, and this one here, with her scarf draped over her shoulders, her garish earrings, and a hairdo straight out of *Vogue*, was definitely from Paris.

"What bag?" she answered curtly.

"A brown leather bag with a zipper and a locking clasp."

"I came on at five, and I haven't seen any bags," the waitress said. She sounded almost happy about it. "You want to order something?"

"A cup of tea, please," Gisèle said, caught off guard.

"Milk? Lemon?" There was a touch of exasperation in the waitress's voice.

"No, thank you. But would you be so kind as to go and check . . . about the bag?"

The waitress bustled about behind the bar, took out a cup, and slammed it noisily onto a saucer. To Gisèle's great chagrin, she dropped a tea bag into the cup and filled it up with hot water. "Twelve francs," she announced as she set the mixture down in front of Gisèle, whose stomach turned at the sight of the chalk-colored foam floating on the surface.

"Could you ask about the bag, please?" Gisèle repeated. But she had to wait a good ten minutes. Two regulars had just come up to the bar, and the waitress, all smiles, rushed over to chat with them and serve them their drinks. The smoke from their cigarettes, a smell Gisèle could scarcely stand, curled over in her direction and made her eyes sting.

At long last a woman who was clearly the owner's wife appeared from behind the bar and walked up to Gisèle. "So you claim to have left a bag," she began in an aggressive tone.

Suddenly overcome with anger, Gisèle forgot for a moment her shyness and the embarrassment of her situation. "I'm not claiming anything at all," she retorted. "Émilienne Robichoux, whom I'm sure you know, left my bag in your care this morning."

"We are not in the business of checking people's luggage, mademoiselle," the woman replied. "If someone agreed to look after your bag, it was to do you a favor, and as far as I know —" She broke off abruptly. "What time did you say you left your bag?"

"Around one o'clock."

"Oh, well, then it wasn't this morning, it was this afternoon," said the proprietress, overjoyed to have found a means of putting Gisèle in the wrong. "It was lunchtime; we were swamped. Wait a minute."

But the minute lasted a quarter of an hour. Gisèle's tea, of which she couldn't bring herself to take so much as a sip, had grown stone-cold. Finally, the proprietress, visibly puzzled, reappeared with empty hands. "My husband says he has a vague memory that someone gave a bag to Albert, one of our part-timers," she said sheepishly. "But we have no idea where he put it. We've looked for it everywhere. And Albert lives in Lamousse, which isn't exactly around the corner."

"Doesn't he have a telephone?" asked Gisèle in desperation.

The woman repressed a shrug, but seeing Gisèle's distraught face, she softened her tone. "God only knows where Albert is at this hour," she explained. "But he's sure to come by tomorrow morning. If you could come back then —" Something occurred to her all of a sudden that made her knit her brows. "Say, there wasn't anything valuable in that bag, was there?"

"Oh, no, not really, just some papers," Gisèle stammered as she slipped off the stool. "I'll come back tomorrow." She could barely manage a whisper. "Thank you . . ."

Gisèle disappeared before the woman had a chance to ask where she could reach her in the unlikely event that Albert would turn up before the next morning. "What a hullabaloo over a few worthless papers!" she grumbled. Scarcely had the bothersome young woman stepped out when a distinguished-looking gentleman took her place at the bar, ordered a kir, and struck up a conversation with the woman in which he complemented her so flatteringly on the way she managed her establishment and commiserated with her so eloquently on the difficulties of running a small business that without even thinking about it, she opened up and told him every detail about her problem with the customer who had been sitting in his place a moment before.

11

DETECTIVE DJEMANI tried to keep her impatience from getting the better of her by tapping softly on the steering wheel to the beat of her favorite blues band. An accident at the Chartres exit had backed up traffic on a ten-mile stretch of the highway from Paris to Orléans, and there was no telling how long it would be before the jam would clear up. Automobile accidents were always accompanied by a number of serious aftereffects to which the public at large was generally oblivious: an increase in the number of heart attacks, a rise in domestic violence, not to mention the inevitable string of minor accidents caused by motorists who, fascinated by the red flashing lights of the ambulances and the strident wail of the sirens, slowed down or came to a full stop in order "to see."

As a trainee, Detective Djemani had worked in several different bureaus, and automobile accidents figured among her worst memories. For reasons that she did not quite understand, all the horror of lethal accidents was summed up for her in the image of a blue stuffed bear

whose head had been severed from its body when a car
traveling at over eighty miles an hour had collided with a
truck on a highway outside Paris. None of the five occupants of the passenger car, which had to be pried off the
bottom of the truck's trailer, were immediately identifiable. The truck driver, dazed, his arm fractured, blood
streaming from a wound on his forehead, kept on saying
that it wasn't his fault. And it wasn't. Like so many other
drivers, the husband and father who was at the wheel of
the car that day had had one drink too many, and he had
suddenly lost control over his vehicle. Five lives cut short in
a split second of carelessness. Leila did her best not to
dwell on the image of the stuffed bear, but she had a hard
time understanding such abuse: of alcohol, of tobacco, of
speed, of power. To her, any abuse that could cause someone to lose control over his own actions was infinitely
more dangerous than anything she was called on to do in
her chosen profession. She had spent her entire childhood trying to preserve order in the chaos that surrounded her: precipitous moves, screaming brothers and
sisters, her father's unannounced absences, her mother's
lamentations . . .

Enshrouded in noxious exhaust fumes, her car inched
forward at a snail's pace. At this rate she wouldn't get there
before midnight, and there were still a number of questions to go over with her superior, for whom she had prepared, thanks to modern technology, a complete dossier
on the victim, Adeline Bertrand-Verdon. Wasn't it amazing
that by pushing a few keys on a computer, one could get
the entire life of a person to come out, black on white, in
neatly aligned columns, from day one to yesterday? How
did they ever manage in the old days? she wondered.

She was too young to know, but not so young that the
question didn't occur to her. She had been lucky enough

to have Mlle Charpentier as her sixth-grade teacher at one of the best high schools in Paris, where she had been accepted into a much-touted pilot program. She had graduated with honors a year ahead of her class and had been a law major in college, where she finished her degree in record time while supporting herself as a waitress, secretary, messenger, baby-sitter, and dancer. The "Bedouin," as her nastier classmates called her because of her dark complexion, hair, and eyes, had gone on to ace the entrance exam to the police academy — and to confront new and more subtle forms of discrimination, this time because she was a woman. Whenever the situation became unbearable, she would recite to herself the words that her history teacher had quoted to her one afternoon after school: "It was Eleanor Roosevelt, Leila, who said that insults debase those who proffer them, not those at whom they are aimed." She wrote every Christmas to Mlle Charpentier, from whom she had learned that for certain people, anything could become a motive for murder: an insult, a few grams of heroin, despair. "You've got everything going for you, Leila. You have two arms, two legs, and a good head on your shoulders, and it's up to you to see to it that it gets the knowledge it needs. You can do anything, be anything you want, go anywhere you like. . . ." Yes, but what would she have to go through to get there?

Keeping to the left of the housing projects clumped on the outskirts of southern Paris, Leila managed to slip onto an access road that would lead her to the smaller routes running parallel to the highway. Anything was better than that congestion. . . . The huge buildings, lit up in spots, rose up beside her like enormous, ghostly fences. She could make out nothing in the dark but these immense rhombus-shaped masses. Still, there was a world of difference between the relative comfort of these suburbs and the abject poverty of the northern outskirts of Paris, where she had grown up. She was suddenly reminded of the night when she had been ripped from her sleep by the noise of the police cars come to announce her father's death: the lights going on all over the neighboring buildings, the children, she among them, pulled from their beds, unable to understand the tragedy that had beset them. Amidst the unspeakable horror of that night, the image of the tall, blond, nameless woman in the blue uniform stood out in her memory. She had bent down to talk to Leila, given her something to drink, comforted her. She was the one, in the end, whose influence had caused Leila to become what she now was: a tall, brown-haired woman in a blue uniform who would bend down to a girl in need, talk to her, give her something to drink, comfort her.

In an effort to block off this unwelcome tide of memories, Detective Djemani tried to concentrate on the dossier she was carrying to Inspector Foucheroux. She smiled involuntarily when she thought of how he would react to what she had found. She had been working with him for three years, and she could tell in a flash what kind of mood he was in by the tone of his voice, what his suspicions were by the way he unconsciously raised his left eyebrow, how tired he was by the way he rubbed his left knee. He could read her mind just as easily as she could his, and the two were linked by a nonverbal communication so fantastic that there was scarcely a suspect who could hold out for long against their combined efforts. They also knew how to exploit the effect of surprise they produced together: he, the well-dressed, middle-aged deputy inspector, exuding good-mannered politeness; she, his detective, clearly a "foreigner," tall as a model, with a demeanor that would never quite mature beyond that of an adolescent. He came from an upper middle-class family in Bordeaux; she was born on the rue Myrrha in north Paris. He couldn't bear to listen to anything but Mozart, Mahler, and a few obscure operas; she liked jazz and blues. He outfitted himself in the most fashionable shops on the Champs-Élysées; she bought her clothes in the flea market at the Clignancourt Gate. And everything else to match. It was a wonder that they could work together at all. Or rather, it was a stroke of genius on the part of their boss, Charles Vauzelle. Right after the riots in the northern outskirts of Paris.

She would never forget the instant when she had been forced to choose. A group of young North Africans had been shattering shop windows to protest the arbitrary arrest of one of their comrades. By the time the police had arrived at the scene, it was too late: the crowds were panicked; three cars were burning in an ill-boding blaze; shadowy figures were darting about, shouting orders to one another in a guttural language she recognized — her own. She had seen the knife emerge from the young man's pocket, seen its long blade, hard and shiny, lunge dangerously toward the throat of her colleague in uniform. She called out. She fired. The young man fell.

She had chosen sides. She had followed standard procedure. She had betrayed her origins.

The threats that she had received afterward bothered her less than the nightmare that woke her, night after night. It was like a moving picture in slow motion: she called out; she fired; the young man fell. The sensational trial that followed would have put her picture on the first page of the newspapers if Charles Vauzelle had not intervened. At the time she looked at it as some sort of disciplinary measure: she was being demoted. They were assigning her to be the nanny of an inspector who had finally deigned to return to active duty after a long sick leave. But in reality her fury had had another cause: the door closed on her for good by her own family, the door to the squalid housing projects on the outskirts of Paris, where her mother, three of her brothers, and her youngest sister eked out a precarious existence. She was a banished woman, a traitor who had refused to wear on her forehead the blue mark of her race. . . .

Forcing her thoughts back to Adeline Bertrand-Verdon, Leila wondered how long it had been since the woman had broken off contact with her family. According to the file, her father had been a bank clerk and was now retired, her mother was a traditional housewife, her brother was a veterinarian, and a sister had become a social worker. Seen from the outside, everything seemed well under control in the uneventful life of this French family, nestled in a typical house in suburbia. What was Adeline Bertrand running away from? She had married an insurance agent when she was twenty and gotten divorced a few months later. Then she had gone back to school, financing herself by giving voice lessons and by laying siege to a number of old, wealthy gentlemen by means of whom she had climbed slowly but surely up the crowded social ladder to a point from which, up until yesterday, she could lay claim to the hand of a viscount. . . .

Leila believed that the key to any mystery could always be found in the way a person had reacted to the humiliations experienced in childhood. Often there was a revolt against one's own class origins that could take any number of forms, snobbism being only the most deplorable: the wish to live elsewhere, to have been born to another family. . . . As though any kind of mediocrity were to be preferred to one's own.

Leila did not usually allow her speculations to roam so far afield at the start of a new investigation on the basis of a few facts. But the Bertrand-Verdon case had stirred up some still waters in her own mind, revived old fears, opened unresolved questions in her past. Leila herself didn't quite know why. "To find the murderer, you have to understand the victim," Jean-Pierre Foucheroux had told her time and again. And Leila understood only too well this woman who seemed to have no friends but who knew a great number of people in high places, who seemed to have succeeded in the eyes of the world but would not be mourned by her family, who wanted desperately to be accepted in a sphere from which the accident of birth had excluded her from the very start. Escape, no matter what from, was still escape, and the stubborn refusal to be left out was the motive of many a violent crime. In order to belong to the in-group, to the forbidden clan, to the upper crust, Adeline Bertrand-Verdon had stopped at nothing. And just as she was about to reach her goal . . . Leila sighed. "We all have our Guermantes," Jean-Pierre Foucheroux had told her once, jokingly quoting the only member of his family who had actually read Proust's withering portrayal of that fictitious aristocratic clan, the object of such misplaced envy. He had no way of knowing then that they would themselves soon be involved in investigating the murder of the president of the Proust Association. . . . The Guermantes in his own life were his in-laws. And the Guermantes in her life was Foucheroux himself. With the one difference that she never tried to force her way into his sphere, had put up an impermeable barrier between his world and hers, and was comfortable with the tiny space she had made for herself between the milieu she had come from and the one where she would never go. She had a room of her own, situated as much in her own imagination as in the tiny apartment she rented next to the gare de Lyon, in the middle of Paris.

*

Inspector Foucheroux had just finished questioning the last of three witnesses, none of whom, he was certain, had told him the truth, and he was not in the best of moods. He gazed in puzzlement at the pages of his notebook, covered with dates, places, and abbreviations that only he could decipher — with the exception, perhaps, of Detective Djemani. He wondered how long he would have to wait before a thread of meaning would emerge from the tangle of scribblings and put him on the track.

His return to the Old Mill Inn had provoked an anxious glare from the owner and his wife, who clearly felt that a police car permanently parked in the courtyard of their "charming country inn" would not be good for business. The stone-cold dinner they had served him in his room was scarcely edible. Was this their way of dissuading him from staying longer than absolutely necessary? Whatever the intended result, the meal had given him indigestion, and he had needed to drink an entire bottle of mineral water to get rid of the bad taste of a so-called sauce forestière.

He had just put another log on top of the bits of willow, pine, and poplar crackling joyously in the fireplace when Patrick Lester Rainsford knocked at the door and entered the room with the victorious demeanor of an American who had just learned that the dollar was on the rise and that he could count on the unconditional support of his embassy. Rainsford surveyed the salon-cum-interrogation room with an expression that said everything about his opinion of the French police force's methods and choice of office space, held up the note that had been given to him, and waited wordlessly in an affectedly relaxed stance for Foucheroux to offer him a seat. Which the inspector did at once, only to hear in response:

"No, thank you. I prefer to stand. I imagine that this little business will not take up much of our time, *monsieur le détective*." And he leaned nonchalantly on the mantelpiece.

"Inspector," Foucheroux corrected him, wondering whether the error, which might have passed for a simple flaw in the American's command of French, had been intentional. "You'll allow me to sit down in order to take a few notes." He chose one of two comfortable armchairs facing one another across a small table and far enough away from his interlocutor that the professor would have to raise his voice a bit in order to make himself heard. This strategy had several advantages, one of which was to force his adversary to change places. Inspector Foucheroux decided not to beat around the bush. "I'm terribly sorry to have to inconvenience you in this way, but we are trying to reconstruct the whereabouts of Mme Bertrand-Verdon yesterday evening, and several witnesses have indicated" — he flipped through three pages of his notebook — "that you were among the last to have seen her, M. Rainsford. Exactly when did you take leave of her?"

Patrick Rainsford's open gaze disappeared for an instant behind lowered eyelids, announcing to Inspector Foucheroux that a lie was about to cross the professor's pretty lips. "Here, of course, in the dining room. There was a dinner for the members of the board of the Proust Association, and I had been invited to join them."

Foucheroux admired the skill with which the professor had evaded his question, but he was not one to be fooled by the strategies of rhetoric. "And what time was the dinner over?" he persisted.

"Oh, at about ten. Twenty-two hours, as you would say in France —"

"Exactly," the inspector commended him in the tone of a schoolteacher praising an average student who had finally given a correct answer. "And how did you leave Mme Bertrand-Verdon?"

"How? What do you mean?" asked Professor Rainsford, visibly piqued. He was not used to being addressed in such a tone.

"On what terms, in what state of mind?" Foucheroux explained, although he was sure that this American had a better ear for the nuances of the French language than many a Parisian whom he had interrogated.

"Oh, well, I thanked her for her kind invitation, said good evening, and went back to my room." He paused. "I'm still suffering from jet lag," he added, thinking it was a good thing to say under the circumstances.

"I see. And what did she say then?"

"She wished me a good night and said that the next day promised to be an interesting one." Was it an illusion? Professor Rainsford seemed suddenly much less relaxed. His voice betrayed a poorly concealed impatience.

"And she seemed —"

"Normal, Inspector, perfectly normal, at least as far as I can make any judgment at all about someone whom I had met socially only once or twice before. You will appreciate, I'm sure, that I am not able to expand on her state of mind." His voice took on an uncontrolled edginess, and his irritation was becoming obvious. "I left her in the company of the members of the board. You'll have to ask them."

"And that is precisely what I intend to do, M. Rains-ford. But if we may stay for a moment with the events of yesterday evening: you are saying, is that right, that you saw Mme Bertrand-Verdon for the last time just before ten o'clock, in the dining room, in the company of Messrs. Verdaillan, Desforge, and de Chareilles?" Patrick Rains-ford nodded briefly and crossed his arms on his chest as though to defend himself from the blows of some imagi-nary assailant. "I see. And lastly: what kind of relationship did you have with Mme Bertrand-Verdon?"

"An entirely professional one, Inspector!" Patrick Rainsford retorted vociferously. "I met her two or three years ago in Washington. When she heard that I was in Paris last week and that I would be attending the conven-tion of the Proust Association, she invited me along with about twenty others to an afternoon tea with chamber music at her apartment. And I saw her yesterday evening, here, at dinner. Our 'relationship,' as you put it, went ex-actly as far as that."

The vehemence with which Patrick Rainsford denied "knowing" the victim seemed curiously incongruous. Foucheroux was reminded of a line from *Hamlet* — or was it *Othello*? — "Methinks thou doth protest too much." But it did seem as though no one wanted to admit to having "known" Adeline Bertrand-Verdon, Foucheroux thought to himself. He put out one last probe. "And your reasons for attending the convention —"

"Listen, Inspector, I believe I have been more than co-operative with your . . . investigation, but I really do not see how I can be of any further assistance," the professor objected. "I'm feeling quite tired and would like to retire for the night."

"Oh yes, the jet lag," murmured Foucheroux. "We can adjourn until tomorrow, of course. But before I let you go, can you tell me whether there is anyone else you saw or spoke with after taking leave of Mme Bertrand-Verdon yesterday evening?"

Professor Rainsford hesitated for a moment and ran his hands through his hair. "No, no one. As I told you, I went straight back to my room. Which is what I would like to do now, if you would allow —"

He's going to threaten me with a lawyer, and with an American lawyer at that, thought Foucheroux. He decided to adopt a more conciliatory tone. "But of course. Thank you most kindly for your help. Few witnesses are as perceptive of details and nuances as you, I must say — it's doubtless due to your experience in literary analysis."

There was no irony intended in this last remark, and Foucheroux was more than a little surprised by the reaction it drew from the American professor. "My field is not literary analysis but critical theory, Inspector," he flung back furiously as he walked to the door. "And since I have an article to finish before the end of the month, I really don't have any time to waste, especially since there's no secretary here to —" He broke off suddenly, his hand already poised to open the door, and turned around to face Foucheroux, who had gotten up out of his chair. "I just remembered," he went on caustically, "last night, when I was going back to my room, I saw Mme Bertrand-Verdon's secretary on the staircase."

"Gisèle Dambert?" asked the inspector.

"As far as I know, she had only one secretary. She was just walking out of the president's room as I walked by." And with that Parthian shot Professor Rainsford vanished, leaving Inspector Foucheroux fully perplexed.

12

WHEN SHE WALKED OUT of the Café de la Gare, Gisèle Dambert felt so weak that she could scarcely make it far enough to collapse onto the bench she had sat on that same morning, with Émilienne. The scene around her had changed. Darkness had closed in, swallowing the harsh winter sun. In front of her, the little lamp suspended above the entrance to the tiny station shone weakly. To her left the avenue de la Gare lay in a jumble of shadows and spots of artificial light emanating from the lampposts that stood at regular intervals. Across from the lighted panes of the café, a dark and empty house stood threateningly, its jagged silhouette rising up out of a garden at the back of which one could just make out a tumbledown ruin.

Gisèle felt caught in a trap. She shuddered, torn between the need to go back to the Old Mill Inn and the desire to retreat to her apartment in Paris to get a hold of herself. She wondered if Katicha would forgive her a second night out. She had her ways — generally fragrant ones — of venting her discontent. . . . Gisèle's physical and mental exhaustion dulled her senses. She wasn't even cold. She was obsessed by a single idea: to recover the lost notebooks, which meant she had to find her bag. A part-time waiter was the only one who could tell her where it was. And no one knew where he was. She didn't even want to think about the other possibilities. She consoled herself with the thought that she had only to wait for "Albert" to get back, and everything would return to normal. She seriously considered spending the night on the bench to be sure not to miss his return.

"Those notebooks are a curse!" she said to herself. They had already caused several deaths. She remembered bitterly the feeling of pure joy that had come over her when she had discovered them by accident, and the gratitude she had felt toward Évelyne, who from beyond the grave had given her a new start and spurred her on to get back to work. Feverishly, Gisèle had deciphered the pages covered front and back with Proust's convoluted handwriting. Between the black cardboard covers she had found the confirmation of her thesis on the genesis of Proust's novel, proof that a key episode in *Remembrance of Things Past* derived from a personal experience of the author as a young man and was not, as scholars had always assumed, a late addition. The young aristocrat whom Proust had taken as a model for the character Albertine was named several times in the notes Proust had scribbled in the margins. Évelyne had bequeathed to Gisèle the means of causing a revolution in Proustian studies and of securing her own future status in research and in the university.

How naive she had been to tell Adeline Bertrand-Verdon about it! But how could she have suspected just how intrinsically low and deceitful the president of the

Proust Association could be? She remembered their first conversation about it all too well. Adeline had asked her, offhandedly, between two thankless clerical tasks: "So, Gisèle, how are you coming along with your thesis?"

"All right, but the next-to-last notebook of 1905 is giving me trouble," she had answered unthinkingly.

Adeline had looked up brusquely from the papers piled up on her desk. "The next-to-last notebook of 1905 —," she said again with alarming slowness. "But it's not in the Bibliothèque Nationale —"

"Uh . . . no, it isn't. It's in a private collection I'm consulting at home." Gisèle had hoped that would be the end of it, but she didn't yet know Adeline as well as she would later. Adeline had pouted like a spoiled child, insisted, wheedled, hinted that she would be of great help in deciphering questionable readings, and hadn't given Gisèle a moment's rest until, on a cold March morning, Gisèle finally gave in and showed her the notebook. She should have known what was coming when she saw the look of diabolical envy that emerged momentarily from behind the expressionless mask her employer was trying to maintain.

"Yes, indeed. At first sight this could really have been written by Marcel Proust," she said evenly. "But there are so many counterfeits. . . . We'll have to consult an expert. Where did you get it? Have you spoken to anyone about it?"

"I was planning on telling Professor Verdaillan, my doctoral advisor, about it, but he's out of town and I haven't been able to get an appointment to see him."

"It's just as well, Gisèle," said Adeline, tapping her chin lightly with a long, polished fingernail. "Guillaume is such a dear, but you know as well as I that he can be a bit stubborn. On the other hand, someone like Philippe, at

Martin-Dubois Press, could be a great help when it comes time to publish. I'll just give him a call —"

"I would prefer to finish my thesis first," Gisèle said feebly, alarmed at the turn things were taking.

"Be reasonable, Gisèle. Everyone knows how it is to write a thesis," said Adeline, who had started work on three different topics, never to get past the second page of the introduction. "But very few people are given the privilege of editing the unpublished manuscripts of a great author." She spoke as though she were scolding a rebellious child. "Let me see what I can do." And with that, she had seized the notebook and vanished before Gisèle could utter a word of protest.

Undeniably, that morning had marked the beginning of a new relationship between the two women. Adeline had blown hot and cold, treating Gisèle sometimes like a friend, sometimes like a servant, leaving her in the dark as to the reasons for her abrupt changes in mood. Up until the evening of the extortion. In early September Gisèle had announced to Adeline — somewhat apprehensively — that she had finished her dissertation and planned to give everything to Professor Verdaillan so that she could schedule a date for her defense. Contrary to what she expected, Adeline hadn't objected at all: she had congratulated her and asked merely to see the other notebooks. Gisèle hesitated just long enough to confirm Adeline's supposition. "Besides, it would give me a chance to proof your manuscript before you give it to your adviser," she suggested amicably. "As you know, I have an eagle's eye for typos. Let's see, why don't I just accompany you home this evening?. . ."

It was the first and last time that Adeline Bertrand-Verdon entered Gisèle's apartment on the rue des Plantes.

107

Katicha had such a violent reaction — hairs raised, eyes bulging, terrifying hisses — that Gisèle had to lock her up in her room for the whole visit.

"You have charming furniture," Adeline remarked. "It would look better in a larger space, of course. Did you inherit it all?"

"Not exactly. It was left to me by a friend, an elderly lady I once knew."

"I see. The same elderly lady that put you onto the notebooks, I'll bet," she murmured, thinking out loud.

"Évelyne knew Céleste," Gisèle answered curtly.

"Évelyne?"

"Évelyne Delcourt. She . . . passed away last year." The sound of the name conjured up for Gisèle the image of the powdered face, the periwinkle-blue eyes, and the benevolent smile of her "adopted grandmother," putting a lump in her throat and pushing her for a moment to the verge of tears.

"Évelyne d'Elcourt. The name sounds familiar," Adeline went on, oblivious to Gisèle's sudden emotion. "No relation to the d'Elcourts of Courbois, I suppose?"

"I don't think so," Gisèle said softly. "She was a piano teacher."

"Oh!" said Adeline, who had already lost all interest in this insignificant person. "Well then, this is where you work. Show me everything, Gisèle." And Gisèle had stupidly gone and opened the secretary, taken out the fifteen notebooks, shown Adeline the six hundred carefully typed pages of her thesis. With a slight smack of her tongue, Adeline sat back and made herself comfortable on the sofa.

"You've made copies?"

"Not of the originals, of course, but of my thesis — I've got everything on diskette."

"Very prudent. But on the other hand, Gisèle, it's pure

folly to keep these manuscripts here. Even putting aside the possibility of a robbery — although you never know, especially in a neighborhood like this, so close to the outskirts — there's still the danger that the paper could deteriorate, that the ink could fade from exposure to bright lights. . . . Not to mention your cat. An accident can happen just like that! No, really, it's not a good idea to store the notebooks under these circumstances. . . . If you had told me about them sooner," she said in a pained tone, "I would have suggested immediately that you keep them in my safe. . . ." Seeing Gisèle recoil instinctively at this idea, she went on, smiling broadly: "You do trust me, Gisèle? Just as I trust you, I who wouldn't hesitate for an instant to give you the combination to the safe if you'd let me take care of these documents for you. Not just for you, but for the whole Proustian community. You have a real treasure there. . . ."

And she had left with the treasure. It was to be the last time Gisèle would see it for several weeks. Up until yesterday evening.

*

Slumped motionless on the bench, which seemed gray in the light of the electric lamp, Gisèle was feeling less and less capable of handling another interview with Inspector Foucheroux. She needed to go home, take off all this makeup, let down this ridiculous hairdo, wash, change, and go to sleep in her bed with Katicha rolled up at her feet. All of a sudden she decided she would go stand at the entrance to the village and catch a ride to Chartres, about eighteen miles away. Then she would get the first train to Paris, take the subway home, and tomorrow . . . Tomorrow, she would see. She could call the Old Mill Inn and the Café de la Gare, come back to the village . . . But right now it was essential that she return to the place where she had survived everything — Évelyne's death, Selim's betrayal, the temptation to commit suicide. She had to get to her apartment on the rue des Plantes. Stiff from sitting still for so long, she walked to the intersection, where a road sign pointed the way to Chartres, and waited. There was not much traffic at this late hour. A truck raced by, followed ten minutes later by two cars with blinding headlights, full of youths on their way to a party. The drivers ignored her raised thumb. Chilled to the bone, she began to walk. She had gone about two miles down the dark and silent road when a van passed her with a loud, mocking honk just as a Renault appeared from the opposite direction. To her astonishment, the Renault braked suddenly and came to a screeching stop. The door opened and a tall, brown-haired woman got out. "Don't you think it's inviting trouble for a lone woman to be hitchhiking on a country road at eleven o'clock at night?" she called out. Underneath the annoyance there was a note of concern — the same concern, Gisèle thought, that she had detected in the voice of Jean-Pierre Foucheroux.

"Inviting trouble," she repeated, "yes, inviting trouble." Fully at nerve's end, Gisèle burst out laughing, then started to sob. The stranger was at her side in an instant. There was a reassuring scent of lime-blossom tea about her, and a healthy warmth. She patted Gisèle gently on the shoulder.

"Come and sit down in my car," she said. "I've got some coffee in a thermos." Gisèle obeyed passively and gulped down the scalding beverage while the young woman gently inquired, "Where were you going?"

"To Chartres station," Gisèle said weakly.

"I'm sorry, but I can't take you there right now. I'm late as it is. Can't you take a taxi?"

"No, I can't. It's a long story . . . ," Gisèle said. Her companion surmised that she didn't have enough money for a taxi or the train.

"Wait until tomorrow," she suggested. "I can't impress upon you enough how dangerous it is to be hitchhiking alone, at night. . . ." She glanced at her wristwatch, then at the map spread out beside her. "Listen, I'm going to the Old Mill Inn, which must be just down the road. Why don't you spend the night there?"

Gisèle took this to be a sign. Caesar's words shot through her mind: *Alea jacta est.* "You're right," she said finally. "It's all I can do. Take the first right, if you would, it's a shortcut. I don't know how to thank you enough for stopping."

"In my profession, prevention is a golden rule, and you learn all too soon to spot people who are in danger," the woman said with a broad smile that brightened up her unfamiliar face.

"Are you a doctor?" Gisèle asked. It seemed likely. She was about Gisèle's age, and there was an assurance in her movements, a seasoned benevolence in her eyes. . . .

"No," she said. "I'm a police detective. And you?"

From the corner of her eye, the woman saw the blood drain from Gisèle's face. Gisèle started to shake uncontrollably, and she grasped instinctively for the door handle, as though to flee.

13

ALONE IN THE SILENCE of his room, where Patrick Lester Rainsford had left him, Jean-Pierre Foucheroux waited for Professor Verdaillan. His knee was hurting. It was one of those moments when it was as painful for him to sit as it was to stand. He did what his surgeon had told him to do in such cases: he lay down flat on his back in front of the fire and tried to relax his muscles as much as possible by controlling his breathing. His gaze slid absent-mindedly along the wooden beams under the ceiling. He saw a knot that looked like an open eye, and a twist in the woodgrain that resembled a pair of outstretched arms.

The smell of the wood fire, of the waxed wooden floor, and of the polish on the furniture reminded him suddenly of the cottage where he had spent his first night with Clotilde, in what was now another life. And before he could put up his internal defenses, the memory of the last night broke in unexpectedly, eclipsing the first. The warmth of carnal love gave way to the bitter cold of the relentless, freezing rain that drenched the stiff corpse of his wife, stretched out next to his own mutilated body on the pavement of a small country road. Jean-Pierre Foucheroux shuddered. He had relived this scene so often, never to reach the limit of its limitless horror, that he knew now to resist what he was about to do: dwell masochistically on all the "if only's," on the lost happiness that nothing now could ever restore, on the guilt that no confession could ever allay.

Wasn't it ironic that he spent most of his time pursuing killers when he himself was a killer, a living, breathing, self-confessed killer? "An automobile accident." He could still hear the calming voice of the psychiatrist. "It was an automobile accident." Accidents happen. One had to accept that. That accidents, by nature, were accidental. "Just as on occasion, rarely but on occasion, a cigar is a cigar." In an effort to reason away his most intimate fears, Foucheroux lay motionless on the floor and began to conjugate the verb *accido*. He had gotten as far as *accidetis* when three knocks at the door cut his Latin drill short. He stood up at once, snapping back into the present, and opened the door for Professor Verdaillan.

"I'm sorry I'm a few minutes late, Inspector," Verdaillan began, taking on an air of importance. "I was talking to my publisher. . . ." At a glance the inspector summed up the real extent of his visitor's nervousness, who, when he was invited to take a seat, sat down without a moment's hesitation in the most comfortable armchair, crossed his legs, and took a cigarette case out of his jacket pocket. "Do you mind?" he said as he lit up. "It's one of my bad habits."

As well as being one of the oldest tricks in the world for hiding one's true thoughts, the inspector said to himself. It keeps your hands busy, gives you time to arrange an answer. . . . Verdaillan seemed to him the perfect caricature of the French academic on the verge of retirement. Bowed shoulders, bifocals, a suit that was a size and a half too small, a pensive air, condescension written all over him, down to the way he held his cigarette — not a single detail was missing.

"Go right ahead. Did Mme Bertrand-Verdon smoke?" he asked, going straight to the subject.

"Well . . . yes, from time to time," Professor Verdaillan answered, caught off guard by the inspector's first question.

"So you knew her well," Foucheroux went on.

Just as he expected, Verdaillan protested vehemently. "No, not at all. We were . . . interested in some of the same things, that's all. I'm the Proust specialist, as you know, and I teach at the University of Paris at Neuilly. She's . . . uh . . . she was the president of the Proust Association. That my path eventually cross hers was only natural."

"And when did they cross for the last time?" the inspector asked, rather put off by the professor's questionable use of the subjunctive mood.

"Yesterday evening, at the dinner held on these very premises for the members of the board. Which is to say Philippe Desforge, M. de Chareilles, and myself. My young American colleague, Professor Rainsford, was also present. But this should not be news to you, since you just spoke with him."

The professor's blatant self-complacency annoyed the inspector, and he decided to show his claws. "True enough. And so far you have confirmed his testimony. But in a criminal investigation the details are what counts, the repetitions, the conflicting versions. In that one way my job resembles yours. And that is why I have to ask you to tell me, as precisely as possible, everything that you have done since arriving at the inn."

114

Professor Verdaillan uncrossed his legs, took a long puff of his cigarette, and looked around in vain for an ashtray before deciding to comply. "I got here around six o'clock yesterday evening. The hotel staff will confirm me on that, Inspector. My wife had planned to come with me, but she fell ill with the flu and had to stay home. So I drove down from Paris by myself, right after I got out of class. The dinner was at eight, and turned out to be most pleasant. I gave a brief summary of my lecture, we went over a few administrative details concerning the business of the Proust Association, talked a little about a number of colleagues, discussed the books on Proust that have just come out. It was more business than pleasure —"

"And how did you find Mme Bertrand-Verdon?"

"Oh, well — true to form, Inspector, true to form. Efficient, very lively. She was overjoyed that the minister of culture and Max Brachet-Léger had both agreed to come to the convention. Of course, at that point, no one could have guessed that both of them would cancel."

"She didn't seem preoccupied about anything? Didn't mention anything about having an appointment after dinner?"

Professor Verdaillan suddenly felt the irresistible urge to get up and throw his half-smoked cigarette into the fireplace. "N-no," he said as he went back to his chair. "I was never to see her again," he sighed. "Early this morning I went to Chartres to check on something in the museum and to gather my thoughts, far away from the crowd, before giving my lecture, which you heard yourself. I didn't hear about what had happened until I got back this afternoon."

"It will be easy enough to confirm all that, as you say," remarked Foucheroux evenly. And looking up from his notebook, he went on: "So you're saying that you saw

Adeline Bertrand-Verdon yesterday evening at the Proust Association dinner, and that you left her —"

"At about ten o'clock. I left her in the company of the other members of the board, and of Patrick Rainsford."

"You were the first to leave?"

Professor Verdaillan paused, seemingly to light up another cigarette. "Yes," he said finally. "It had been a long day, and I wanted to put a few finishing touches on my lecture."

"Quite understandable," mused the inspector amiably. "Unfortunately, what you've told me contradicts the testimony of another witness in one detail. One of you has a faulty memory. I would suggest that you go over everything you've told me before signing your official statement tomorrow. And — I thank you most kindly for your cooperation."

"I had planned on returning to Paris tomorrow morning," said Verdaillan belligerently. "My wife —"

"But there's no reason you shouldn't, I would think, as soon as you've finished with the paperwork," the inspector broke in gently. "Just leave us an address and a phone number where we can reach you in case something comes up we need to ask you about." And with a polite smile, he accompanied the professor to the door and advised him, a touch of irony in his voice, to get some much-deserved rest.

He took advantage of the few minutes before the next appointment to read through his notes. Underneath all the polite restraint and subtle slips of the tongue, a less-than-flattering portrait of Adeline Bertrand-Verdon was beginning to emerge. The dossier that Leila was bringing him would provide a more complete picture of the victim. The victim. Why was he so uncomfortable using this word to describe the president of the Proust Association? Intuitively he had already placed her among the perpetrators. Like a photographer in his darkroom, agitating a print with a pair of tongs in a shallow tub of developer, Foucheroux suddenly recognized the hazy outlines of a blackmailer. But he didn't have time to dwell on the idea, for just then the five-foot-three frame of the associate publisher of Martin-Dubois Press, his hands in his pockets, his eyes evasive, appeared in the doorway. A bit out of breath, he asked in a hollow voice if he could come in.

"I realize what a shock the news of Mme Bertrand-Verdon's death must have given you," Inspector Foucheroux said, a touch of compassion in his voice.

Philippe Desforge's speckled gray suit made him seem even shorter than he really was. He pushed his hands deeper into his pockets and cleared his throat a few times. "Adeline — Mme Bertrand-Verdon — and I were friends . . . ," he whispered, stumbling over the last word.

Lovers, Foucheroux understood intuitively.

"Intimate friends," Desforge went on, somewhat louder now. "Our relationship . . ." He faltered again.

"I can understand how hard this is for you," the inspector broke in, convinced Desforge's grief was genuine. Unless this was the unsurpassed performance of a consummate actor — a possibility that occurred to him, paradoxically, when he heard the candid disclosure that came next.

"I'm a bad liar, as you can see, Inspector. And I'm sure you could have found out about my relationship with Adeline by some other means anyway. I met her two years ago. We were introduced by my wife — my ex-wife, that is. Mathilde Merlot." A bleak smile crossed his face when the inspector let slip an expression of surprise. "I see you know the name. . . ."

He did indeed. The whole country knew the name, the voice, the face of French television's most formidable film and book critic. Being her prince consort couldn't have been an easy job.

"Mathilde had done an interview with Adeline on the meccas of French literature and had invited her to dinner afterward," Philippe Desforge went on. "I met her at our apartment." He paused for a moment, carried away by the memory of this first meeting. "She was so cheerful, so energetic, so witty. . . . Just being with her made me feel ten years younger. Shortly afterward, she called me at the office about one of her literary projects. We had lunch together several times. I visited her in her apartment on the rue Saint-Anselme. That was how the *Guide of the Perfect Proustian* was born. . . ." Foucheroux admired the editor's discreet omission and waited patiently for him to continue. Desforge gave a sigh. "But all that won't be much of a help to you," he went on. "I just wanted to tell you about my . . . uh . . . connection to Adeline before you heard it from someone else."

"You were divorced just a little while ago. . . ."

"There's no keeping secrets from you, Inspector. You're quite right, the divorce was finalized just a month ago."

"That must have freed up your options," Foucheroux concluded, although he could scarcely imagine Adeline, still a young woman, consenting to wed this scraggly little sixty-year-old who could quite easily have been her father. "Tell me, if it isn't too painful, about the last time you saw Mme Bertrand-Verdon."

"It was here, yesterday evening." Suddenly closing his eyes, Philippe Desforge drew a reddish fingertip over his eyelids. "We were having a dinner for the members of the board," he said wearily, "along with Professor Rainsford. It was over at about ten o'clock, when everyone went to bed."

"And you didn't see Mme Bertrand-Verdon . . . later?"

"No!" Philippe Desforge protested, blushing like an adolescent. "Adeline was tired and had told me that she didn't want to be . . . uh . . . disturbed. The last time I saw her was in the dining room of this hotel, in public, in the company of Professor Verdaillan, Professor Rainsford, and M. de Chareilles."

"You're positive about that?" said the inspector, who wanted him to repeat this last statement.

"Absolutely. I was the first to leave the table. Adeline wanted to finish early, and she gave me a signal we'd arranged beforehand when it was time for me to take my leave." He rubbed the fingers of his left hand with the flat of his right and added: "Which is what I'd like very much to do right now, if you would be so kind. . . ." His voice was almost pleading, and his growing anxiety was now obvious in the way he fidgeted with his hands.

Foucheroux didn't have the heart to keep on interrogating the third person who had claimed, in the space of a few hours, to have been the first to leave the dinner table at which Adeline Bertrand-Verdon had presided, yesterday evening, for the last time in her life. He was tired himself, which was doubtless why he didn't give another thought to the association he had when he saw Philippe Desforge leave his room with a sprightlier step and a straighter back than one would have expected from a man overcome with the loss of his lover: the two-faced head of Janus. Janus, whom Saturn had endowed with the extraordinary power of looking simultaneously into the past and into the future . . .

14

THE MOON, WELL INTO ITS LAST QUARTER, shone
dimly on the secluded buildings of the Teissandier family's farm. It was one of those uncomely farms one finds in
the Beauce, sitting squarely in the middle of unendingly
dreary wheat fields that stretch in all directions as far as
the eye can see. Albert had sworn he would break free of
the place as soon as possible. He had just turned eighteen, and there was nothing he wouldn't do to save up
enough money to get to Paris, the first step in what he
hoped would become a trip around the world. That evening he had earned a bundle playing guitar at a local
ball, and the contents of the envelope that he had stashed
carefully in the saddlebag of his moped had already carried him, in his imagination, as far as London, or even
Liverpool.

Albert had the glistening red hair and the perky gaze
of a young cocker spaniel. He whistled as he drove, taking
the familiar turn into the little road leading up to his parents' farm at top speed. Suddenly the headlights of a car

flared up in his path. Momentarily blinded, he felt his moped skid out from under him, and in a great slide of gravel, he found himself facedown on the ground, his elbows skinned and his head more than a little shaken in spite of his regulation helmet, which was supposed to protect it from just such a fall.

As he tried to get up, Albert saw a cloud of little bright spots dancing before his eyes. A foot came down on his chest, pinning him to the ground and cutting off his breath. He could just make out the shadowy outline of a man in a raincoat, a hat pulled down over his eyes and a scarf over his nose and mouth. No doubt about it, he was being mugged just two hundred yards from his own house! The silhouette appeared above him at the center of a web of blinding light, just as he had seen in the dozens of science-fiction movies he had adored as a child. How many times had he dreamed of actually encountering an extraterrestrial being, and of how famous that would make him! But the voice that he heard next was definitely a human one:

"Stay right where you are, Albert. And tell me where you put the bag."

"The bag?" he asked confusedly. "What bag?"

"Don't play dumb with me, Albert," the voice said threateningly. "Tell me where it is, unless you want something worse to happen to you. . . ."

"I don't know what you're talking about," the young man gasped, scarcely able to speak. He was determined not to give up the fruit of his labors so easily to someone he assumed was the leader of a Chartres gang.

"Then let me refresh your memory." And with a vicious kick to his side, which was already bruised black and blue by the fall, Albert's assailant knocked the breath out of him.

"In the bicycle pouch," he stammered as soon as he could speak again. If he really had to choose between his money and his life, he wasn't going to spend a lot of time thinking about it.

"What do you take me for, some kind of moron? How can an overnight bag fit in a bicycle pouch?" Albert felt something cold and hard press against his throat. He was on the verge of panicking when an idea suddenly entered his mind, and in a flash he realized that his attacker was not after his money.

"The bag that Émilienne gave me to keep?"

"Hey, that's right! See, it wasn't so hard to remember after all. . . . Where did you put it?"

Albert was in a state of shock. He tried to sort out in his mind a chain of events that seemed to have occurred light-years away from the present moment. For the first time in his short life, he was afraid of dying. He tortured his aching mouth into pronouncing a few painful words: "I put it behind the counter. By the Italians' bags."

"What Italians?" the voice asked roughly.

"Five Italians. Campers who had come in to eat lunch. Jesus Christ almighty —"

"You lie to me, Albert, and you really will need to say your prayers —"

"But I'm not lying," the young man groaned. "I put the bag that Émilienne gave me behind the counter, next to the Italians' stuff. They were eating lunch before taking the afternoon train to Chartres. I even remember giving them their check before they finished their coffee, because I had to leave at two o'clock sharp."

"You left before they did? You didn't see them go?"

"No, that's what I'm telling you. . . . Oh no!" Suddenly, Albert realized the extent of the disaster. The Italians had taken Émilienne's bag by mistake. Unless they did it on purpose. Unless they had stolen it . . . Apparently his attacker had just had the same thought, for the weight that had been crushing his rib cage since the start of their conversation eased up a bit.

"How did they pay their bill?"

"In cash, and they didn't leave a tip," Albert said miserably, knowing all too well what his assailant was getting at. If they had paid with a check or a credit card, he could track them down. But with cash there was no hope at all.

He heard a muffled curse from out of the darkness, then, right next to his ear, a voice whispering wicked words, branding them in fiery letters into his memory: ". . . we understand each other now, don't we, Albert? You had an accident, just an accident, when you took the curve too fast. Otherwise —" Unable to move a muscle, Albert kept hearing the same wicked words shoot through his wavering consciousness, until a violent chop to his throat just below his Adam's apple plunged him into a welcome void.

*

The wind must have picked up again. Sitting in front of the fire that had threatened repeatedly to fizzle out, Jean-Pierre Foucheroux nursed a near-empty snifter of Armagnac and waited for Detective Djemani to arrive. It was a rare occasion. Since the accident he hardly ever drank, never smoked, and ate without ever being hungry, just to survive.

"Clotilde," the little flames murmured over and over, dancing above the logs in the fireplace. "Clotilde." It was in the winter that he had heard her name for the first

123

time. His older sister was giving a fondue party and had insisted that he come. "At eight o'clock, Jean-Pierre." So-and-so would be there — he had forgotten the other names — as well as "Clotilde de Clairmonteil."

The first name conjured up in his mind the image of a Merovingian princess with braided hair in ancient attire, a being who wouldn't walk but hover. And when he saw her, that evening — perched, smiling, on a high-backed chair, with her hair done up in a sort of crown — what he saw was not the young psychology student who was his sister's friend but "Chilpéric's daughter," the daughter of the king in the fairy tale printed next to his favorite illustration in the gilt-edged book with the red cover and the mysterious title, the one that he read and reread every night before going to sleep, when he was a child. . . . She looked up at him with her clear blue eyes. Unthinkingly, she let her forefinger rest for a moment at the corner of her full lips and swung her slender foot a bit from side to side, causing the slit on the side of her velour skirt to fall open. Two years later, Clotilde de Clairmonteil became Mme Jean-Pierre Foucheroux. Engraved in gilded letters on the black marble of her tombstone now stood, "Here lies Clotilde Foucheroux-Clairmonteil. . . ."

"Clotilde, Clotilde," the flying sparks sang out over and over in a strange chant. And Foucheroux, so often the victim of insomnia, dozed off like a newborn babe until a knock on the door roused him from a dreamless slumber. Leila Djemani had arrived.

When she saw the distress on his face as he opened the door, she immediately thought: Clotilde. Behind them a perturbed Gisèle Dambert stood by as they exchanged the knowing glance of two friends just rejoined, the kind that Gisèle herself used to exchange with Évelyne, excluding the rest of the world. Her, in this case. Now they were two against one.

"Mlle Dambert has something she wants to tell you," Leila Djemani said simply as she walked into the dimly lit room.

"At this hour of the night?" remarked Inspector Foucheroux sardonically as he regained his chair. "Come in, mademoiselle. I'm all ears. Have a seat, if you like," he added, gesturing toward a sofa near the fireplace.

"I wanted . . . I needed to tell you that I didn't go back to the hotel after the conference was over. . . ." Seated behind her right shoulder, Detective Djemani had noiselessly taken out her black notebook.

Foucheroux asked the obvious question. "And where did you go?"

"To the Café . . . the Hôtel de Guermantes, that is."

"There's nothing wrong with that," the inspector remarked in a conciliatory tone.

"No, there isn't," said Gisèle, looking down. "But afterward, I . . . I decided to go back to Paris. I wanted to call you tomorrow morning . . . this morning . . . or to come back. . . ." Leila Djemani coughed. "The last train for Chartres had already left," Gisèle went on. "I tried to hitchhike. . . . Detective Djemani picked me up."

"I see," said Foucheroux. Gisèle hated the sound of these two words. He was a master of innuendo.

Leila coughed again and excused herself. "A frog in my throat," she said.

But the interruption did nothing to divert the inspector from his next question. "And how long did you stay at the Hôtel de Guermantes?"

"Oh, not long. Less than an hour."

"Less than an hour. And then?"

"Then I sat on a bench outside. And then I walked to the edge of town in order to hitchhike —"

"You sat on a bench for three hours?" he said in disbelief. He exchanged glances with Leila, who gave a slight shrug. Each of them knew instantly what the other was thinking. A moment later, Leila heard the inspector say the exact words she was expecting to hear next:

"Listen, Mlle Dambert, it's late and we're getting nowhere. Why don't we all sleep on it? You need some rest anyway. We'll take this up again tomorrow as planned, but a little later. Here, at eleven."

"Odd customer," remarked Leila Djemani as soon as the door had closed behind Gisèle. "Here's the file on Bertrand-Verdon," she added, handing him a red folder. "I'll be in the annex, in room seven, if you need me." And with a polite "Good night, Inspector," she was gone. He was grateful to her for knowing without his having to say so that he preferred to be alone.

Along with the red folder, she had also brought him his revolver, discreetly wrapped in a little black box.

15

A GRAY AND FRIGID DAWN ushered in a windy morning that did nothing to entice even the English Proust scholars, who were used to the fogs and chills of the British Isles, to take advantage of the excursion scheduled for that morning. After the continental breakfast served from seven o'clock on in the rustic dining room of the Old Mill Inn — coffee, croissants, baguettes with butter, and madeleines (in honor of the occasion) — two dozen of the more faithful conventioneers filed into the Tourist Office's old bus and were carted off to admire, from a distance, the Tansonville estate and the Saint-Éman wash basin, or, in the words of Proust's novel, "the Swann house" and "the liquid portal to the Underworld." In deference to the touchy puritanism of certain British and American members of the association, the organizers had elected to leave out a visit to the slope where, under the flimsily disguised name of "Montjouvain," Proust had chosen to situate the first great voyeuristic and sadistic scene of his long novel.

Professor Rainsford had decided to come along as well, partly because it was an excellent way to avoid Inspector Foucheroux, and partly because of the remote possibility he would meet the rich American lady who had bought the Tansonville estate and persuade her to take a — financial — interest in the growth of his Center for Postmodern Manuscripts.

Sadly, the little group was greeted at the white garden fence by a young man who informed them that he could by no means allow anyone to visit the house, as the owners were not in. But he added graciously that he would, on this one occasion, allow them to take pictures. The daylight was so minimal that few of the visitors bothered to waste their film. Nevertheless, two or three devotees posed for their companions in the lifeless garden, while others took a few quick shots of the main house. But most of them sat huddled up in the bus and listened to a young woman enlisted that very morning by André Larivière read, rather haltingly, selected excerpts from *Combray* on the subject of Tansonville. Unfortunately, she got the page numbers mixed up and treated her listeners to the passage about the hawthorns and other descriptions of Swann's park, all of which were in fact based on the Pré Catelan, which had belonged to Proust's uncle and was now a public park situated two or three miles down the road.

This was where the bus stopped next, at the entrance to the "Garden of Marcel Proust, national historic site designated by the Ministry of Culture on December 12, 19—" But despite André Larivière's repeated injunctions to "imagine the hawthorn blossoms" as he stood beside a string of barren, shivering hedges, no one ventured onto the frost-covered paths, and no one seemed eager to be recorded for all posterity posing in front of the decrepit pigeon house, the dilapidated little pavilion, or the dried-up fountain. So the group took leave of the fictional "Swann's Way" and drove down some rather poorly paved back roads in pursuit of the equally fictional patch of countryside said to belong to the Guermantes.

On the way there, Patrick Rainsford came up with a plan that would offer him an elegant way out of his current pinch. All he needed was a telephone booth from which to place a collect call to his wife, telling her to send him a telegram requiring his immediate return to the United States. It was four o'clock in the morning on the East Coast, and he thought nothing at all of tearing his wife from the embrace of a deep sleep. She had an unhealthy tendency to sleep like a log anyway. And he had to be called back on some urgent business, that was his only way out. God only knows what this inspector, who was far from being an idiot, was going to turn up in the course of his investigation. He would end up getting the secretary, who was sure to have overheard part of that unfortunate conversation with Adeline Bertrand-Verdon, to talk.

It was better to think ahead. Reluctantly Rainsford gave up on his plan to win over Max Brachet-Léger and decided to forget all the schemes he had wanted to set in motion in the reception halls of the American embassy on the rue Saint-Florentin. The bus trundled along through a landscape of dreary plains and frozen streams the sun had still not managed to thaw. But Rainsford preferred the sight of the wintry desolation that slipped by the foggy pane of the bus window on his left to the slightest interaction with the pilgrims on his right. He abhorred organized tours, and he remembered all too well how confined he had felt during the obligatory visit to the Lycian tombs in Turkey, that summer when he had had to court Jennifer. The memory of the crypts sculpted right into the stone of the mountains of Anatolia brought him back, by simple association, to the death of Adeline Bertrand-Verdon. . . .

He still didn't understand why, after she had quietly asked to see him in the hotel after dinner so that they could put the finishing touches on the announcement of her appointment as associate director of the Center for Postmodern Manuscripts, she had canceled at the last minute. "I have to go to Aunt Léonie's," she had told him curtly. "Wait for me. I'll see you later."

Later, after two hours pacing back and forth in his room trying in vain to reach her by phone, he had snuck out to his rental car and driven to the village, expecting at the very least to meet up with her Alfa Romeo on her way back to the hotel. But he drove all the way to Aunt Léonie's house without seeing a soul. He parked in front of the church, got out of his car, and, hugging the walls, made his way to the entrance of the house. It lay in total darkness, like the other houses in the village, and there was not a sound to be heard. The door was unlocked, and he stole inside. "Mme Bertrand-Verdon?" he called out, in as confident a voice as he could muster. But there was no response. A slender ray of moonlight fell through the pane in the garden door onto the tiles of the hallway floor, painting them an odd pinkish mauve. All the other doors were closed. Suddenly, he thought he heard a board creak upstairs. "Adeline?" he said aloud as he overcame his reluctance and stepped into the staircase, unaware of the allusion to Proust's novel: he had skipped over Marcel's heartbreaking ascent to his bedroom at the opening of *Combray*. When he got to the top of the stairs, he saw a patch of light by a half-open door. "Adeline?" he said again.

Just then, after jolting past an especially ugly cluster of recently constructed houses, the bus stopped in the middle of nowhere by the entrance to the Saint-Éman church, ripping Patrick Rainsford from the abominable memory of his own hand grasping the little plaster statue that had cut short the life of the Proust Association's president.

*

The Saint-Éman church, standing alone in the middle of a little country cemetery, is the repository of the relics of a saint who, when faithfully called upon, will cause a salutary rain to fall on the plains of the Beauce during the scorching months of July and August. But deep in this all too humid November, no one required his services. The little group spread out around the wash basin and stood by wordlessly watching tiny bubbles break the surface of the water as the young woman reeled off the passage from Proust about the basin, *as extra-terrestrial as the gates of hell.*

"At least it's warm in hell," hazarded softly the husband of a rapturous Proust fan. At that point André Larivière suggested they return — after a brief stop at a nearby farm mentioned in one of the earlier versions of Proust's masterpiece — to the hotel, where they could rest up for lunch and for the tour of Aunt Léonie's house itself, which was to take place at two-thirty sharp that afternoon.

Patrick Rainsford asked if it wouldn't be possible to stop in the village long enough to buy postcards. Two or three of the others expressed the same wish, and when the bus stopped on a dreary-looking intersection in front of a café, the American professor was greatly relieved to see the typical glass box of a French telephone booth on the corner. He rushed over to it. Unfortunately, this ultra-modern phone would only work with a telephone card. Furious, he jammed his change back into his pocket and went back to his seat, where he now waited impatiently for the bus to set off for the farm, his last hope. He grumbled to himself about the "tourists" keeping him from his all-important phone call.

"I'd like to make a collect call," he said to the young woman in traditional peasant dress who had taken orders for tea, milk, honey, mulled wine, and grog, as soon as he had a chance to speak to her in private.

"But of course, monsieur," she said, and showed him to a little alcove next to the bathroom, where an old black phone was mounted on the wall between a broom and a sack of rags.

Never in his life had he been so happy to speak to an operator, although she made him repeat Jennifer's name, his own name, and his phone number three times. "Just a moment, please." He heard a series of clicks, and the line went totally silent. The wait seemed endless, and he gave a start when the operator finally came back on the line: "No answer, sir."

"What do you mean, no answer?"

"There's no answer. The party does not respond."

She's asleep, he thought. And he went livid with anger as he thought of his lawful wife lying peacefully asleep thousands of miles away, her face glistening with moisturizing cream, a few curlers in the blond locks just beginning to show a touch of gray, a cloth mask covering her eyes, her ears stopped up with little foam plugs. Either that or she wasn't home. At her parents'? At her twin sister's? Somewhere else? Somewhere else . . . Suddenly, Rainsford had a disturbing vision of another, provocative, madeup Jennifer, asleep in someone else's bed. . . .

"— try again later," the impersonal voice of the operator was saying.

"Yes, I'll try again later," he said and hung up. It took him several minutes to rid his mind of the grotesque suspicion that had just taken hold of him. And to think up another way of carrying out his plan.

"Hi, Bob!" A quarter of an hour later he had his brother on the phone, dumbfounded at having been awakened by a call from France in the middle of a balmy California night, fresh with the scent of eucalyptus plants. "It's Pat. . . . Listen, Bob, here's what I want you to do. . . ."

His mission accomplished, Patrick Rainsford scarcely noticed the person he bumped into as he left the alcove. Without even bothering to look up, he muttered an unthinking "Excuse me" and went back to join his compatriots, who had been miraculously transformed into a jolly little crowd by the alcoholic beverages sitting on the tables in front of them.

*

Long before the small congregation of Proustians had vanished into the morning mists, Inspector Foucheroux and Detective Djemani were already hard at work. As soon as she arrived in the "torture chamber," as they began to call the inspector's curious little sitting room, Leila could see that Foucheroux had completely pulled himself together again and recovered his customary professional manner and tone of voice. Clean-shaven, his hair damp but groomed, a cup of coffee in his hand, he looked like a modern version of Saint Michael armed to slay the dragon, although the little wrinkles at the corners of his gray eyes and around his mouth betrayed a sleepless night.

They compared notes and first impressions. And they agreed not to draw up a definitive list of suspects until they had the results of the autopsy and of the other laboratory reports. "As usual, every one of them has

133

something to hide," sighed Foucheroux. "That's why they contradict one another. But I've never before heard the same lie repeated three times in a row by three different people, each time with the same conviction. . . . As for what they did afterward . . ." He broke off in midsentence.

"We have no way of checking their whereabouts after ten o'clock," Leila agreed, "what with three staircases and all of these French windows on the ground floor. Not to mention the parking spaces strategically hidden behind the trees so as not to spoil the view. People come and go here like in a railroad station."

But Inspector Foucheroux was already thinking about something else. "As for Gisèle Dambert —"

Something in his voice made her prick up her ears. "You don't think she's capable of —," she said cautiously.

"You know as well as I that anyone is capable of anything given the right circumstances, which vary from individual to individual," he said bluntly. "God only knows where she'd be now if you hadn't picked her up on the road. She says she spent the night of the crime in her apartment in Paris, but M. Rainsford claims he saw her going out of Adeline Bertrand-Verdon's room after dinner. Why would he be lying?"

"Why would she be lying?" ventured Detective Djemani, deciding to play devil's advocate. "It all depends on your personal definition of 'night.'"

"That's what we're going to have to find out when we talk to her. As well as how she felt about her working conditions as secretary of the Proust Association."

"And would you say that the others also stood something to gain from the disappearance of the president?" asked Leila Djemani, who saw immediately what he was getting at.

"I don't know," the inspector admitted. "In fact, I know

nothing about the motives, or the murder weapon, or even the exact time of the crime. The criminal records people were very efficient, and I have utmost confidence in the medical team, but as long as we don't have the results black on white —"

"The medical examiner has already given you a rough idea," Leila said reassuringly. "And you've finished the preliminary questionings —"

"Which tell us almost nothing. Professor Rainsford emphasized how little he knew Mme Bertrand-Verdon, Guillaume Verdaillan doesn't seem to have had much respect for her, and Philippe Desforge admitted — rather too readily, if you ask me — to having been her lover. And if it's true that M. de Chareilles was thinking about marrying her . . ."

"Aren't we supposed to see him this morning?" she reminded him.

"Yes," he said, vaguely annoyed. "We'll have to call the Château de la Moisanderie to tell them we're coming."

"I'll take care of it if you like," said Leila Djemani.

"Would you?" He glanced approvingly at her attire. She was not in uniform. She was wearing a gray-blue outfit consisting of a knee-length coat and a wool skirt with a matching sweater that had cost her a fortune, even secondhand — but it did come in handy on an occasion like this one — boots, and a black leather purse. Her thick dark hair was held back with a tortoiseshell comb. He knew what an effort it must have cost her to assimilate this way. After the first outward signs of revolt, Leila had gone through a miraculous transformation. The gold-plated, jingling earrings and the multicolored scarfs had disappeared, along with the other vestmental declarations of her "difference." In exchange, she had managed to teach him, by means of a little friendly teasing, to loosen up a little — not to be ashamed of being seen without a tie, for example.

Through the intermediary of his clerical assistant, M. de la Moisandière let them know that he would be unable to receive them before ten-thirty, as his wife Marie-Hélène had made previous engagements, and he himself had some business to take care of at the bank that was of the utmost importance for international finance. The Viscount of Chareilles would be free to see them at around eleven.

16

EVEN BEFORE SHE WAS FULLY AWAKE, Gisèle spotted
the white envelope on the breakfast tray that the chambermaid had just brought in. With a joyous "Good morning, mademoiselle!" the maid threw back both sets of
curtains to reveal an ugly-looking new day. "It'll clear up
in no time," she asserted optimistically, in spite of the
thick fog that blocked everything from view but the contorted branches on the tops of the nearest trees.

Gisèle suddenly remembered the morning when, as a
little girl, she had burst into Yvonne's room, shouting
frantically, "Yvonne, Yvonne, the sky's fallen down!"

"It's fog, Gisèle, fog. Go back to bed," her older sister
had mumbled sleepily.

". . . from the condensation of water vapor that occurs
when a cold mass of air comes into contact with a mass of
warmer, humid air. When the air is saturated with water, a
cloud of fine droplets forms . . . ," their father had explained at great length later at lunch when Yvonne

blamed the rude way she had been torn from her sleep for her ill humor.

Gisèle thanked the chambermaid, who scurried off with a look of bewilderment Gisèle had a hard time accounting for, and contemplated the tray on the round table next to the bed. Two white porcelain pots, one filled with coffee and the other with milk, sat waiting to be emptied into a cup and saucer seated decorously between a basket filled with slices of fresh bread and a vase in which a single rosebud stood, readying itself to bloom. To the left, on either side of the silverware wrapped in a damask napkin, two small ramekins cradled symmetrical portions of butter and preserves. Gisèle diverted her gaze from the appetizing red jam that reminded her all too keenly of her reckless deed, poured herself a cup of coffee, and resolutely opened the envelope that bore her name.

In an elegant style that left no room for equivocation, Inspector Foucheroux informed her that their appointment would have to be postponed once again, to one o'clock in the afternoon, and would take place not in his room but at the police station. Despite what that might imply, Gisèle felt better. She had managed, somehow, to get a few hours of sleep, and now she had been given a reprieve. She dipped a slice of buttered bread into a second cup of coffee and made up her mind to get in touch with Professor Verdaillan, and then to go see what she could find out at the Café de la Gare.

Her watch, a vial of sleeping pills, her contact lenses, and the garish earrings that Ray Taylor had foisted upon her lay in a jumble on the nightstand. What a costume, she thought. The clothes she had worn the night before were dangling pitifully from the arms of a comfortable-looking chair. The sleeve of her blouse hung down in such a way as to conceal the tip of a shoe, making it look strangely like a boat docking on an island.

A shower. The thought of the refreshing water streaming down her deadened limbs drew her to the tastefully decorated bathroom, where she found toothpaste, soaps, shampoo, skin lotion, shoe polish, and a sewing kit, all neatly placed in small ribbon-tied baskets. There was no escaping the mirror, which covered an entire wall of the little room, and she gave herself quite a fright. When she had finally made it to her room the night before, she had been too exhausted even to remove her makeup. She had scarcely had the strength to undress and swallow a sleeping pill before burrowing in between the flowered sheets on the bed. During the night her mascara had run down her face in long, black tears, her makeup had flaked off in little scales, her lipstick had turned orange and spilled over onto her chin, and her hair, tangled in the hairpins she had neglected to take out, stood up on top of her head in jagged tufts, giving her the crazed look of one of the three Gorgons. She went through their names in her head: Medusa, Euryale, and Stheno. No wonder the chambermaid had acted as though she was afraid she'd be turned to stone if she looked Gisèle in the eyes!

Without losing another second, Gisèle jumped into the shower and systematically rubbed, scoured, and rinsed, stoically ignoring the stinging of her eyes and the painful tangles in her hair. After twenty-five minutes of this treatment she wrapped a large bath towel around her combed and straightened hair, draped herself with great relish in the terry-cloth bathrobe that bore the monogram of the hotel, and walked up to the misty mirror to look at her face, cleansed and rosy from the hot water. Aside from the shadowy rings on the delicate skin under her eyes, she was her old self again, at least on the outside. She called the front desk and asked for a hairdryer and an iron.

Reluctantly, Gisèle looked over at the ramekin of preserves, and the thoughts that she had temporarily managed to repress froze her in an uncomfortable position on the edge of the bed. How could she ever explain the white powder that she had mixed into Adeline's rose-petal jam without revealing everything else? How could she explain why she had needed to be absolutely sure that her employer would sleep soundly and would not have the impulse to go back to Paris and spend the night before the convention in her apartment? Gisèle had never intended to kill Adeline, just to put her to sleep long enough to recover what belonged to her, had been stolen from her. . . . And now . . . Now, she scolded herself, you have to go talk to your thesis advisor and then go look for your bag. And above all, above all, she had to swear not to pronounce Yvonne's name. Not to think of Yvonne's name at all, which would lead inevitably to that of Selim.

There was a knock at the door and another chambermaid, rather less fearful than the first, brought her what she had asked for on the phone. Gisèle asked her to deliver a note to Professor Verdaillan, requesting his leave to come and speak with him sometime in the next hour.

*

They met in a little room on the ground floor of the inn that had been set up as a kind of library. There was a crackling fire in the open hearth. As though to counteract the intimate atmosphere of the decor, Verdaillan was at his most professorial. He took his time wiping his glasses and pointed, in a gesture that seemed to forbid any reply, at the chair where Gisèle was supposed to sit.

140

"Yes, Mlle Dambert?" he asked curtly.

Intimidated as she was, Gisèle decided nevertheless to dive right in. "I wanted to let you know what stage my thesis is at —"

"Very good," he said, gazing distractedly at a row of old books on the wall to his right.

"I was hoping I could schedule my defense sometime in the next six weeks, if that would suit your schedule —"

"That depends on . . . a number of things," he said. He sounded less than enthusiastic. "How many pages do you have, and what state are they in?"

"Seven hundred and forty-two, and a final version on diskette. It's all finished."

He gave a little grimace, the meaning of which was not quite clear. "Remind me of the exact title we had agreed upon."

"That's one of things I wanted to ask you about," Gisèle ventured bravely. "With your consent, I had chosen to write on 'Transition in the Work of Marcel Proust,' but in fact I concentrated almost uniquely on the transition between *Jean Santeuil* and *Remembrance of Things Past* —"

"Without consulting me," the professor interrupted sternly.

"I sent you a note at the university last year," the student protested.

"A note I never received, I assure you," he answered brusquely. "Which is scarcely surprising, considering the secretarial staff, or rather the lack of a secretarial staff to which professors in France seem, alas, to be destined."

"I tried to reach you several times, but you were abroad," the young woman continued, holding her ground.

"It's true," he sighed, somewhat mollified. "I have been traveling a lot these last months. . . ." And he enumerated smugly the list of American, African, and East Asian universities that had required his presence in the recent past.

"What I wanted to tell you about," Gisèle went on as soon as he had finished, "was that I've been working on unpublished manuscripts — the notebooks of 1905, to be precise." All of a sudden, the temperature in the room seemed to drop by several degrees. Mechanically, Guillaume Verdaillan took a package of cigarettes out of his pocket, and with a scarcely audible, pro forma "Do you mind?" lit one with a gold lighter, the flame of which trembled markedly.

"And where did you come across these notebooks, may I ask?" There was a note of skepticism in his voice.

"They were entrusted to me by Évelyne Delcourt, a friend of Céleste Albaret. There are fifteen of them. I've made an exact transcription, and my thesis is in fact an interpretation —"

"Legally entrusted?" He seemed to have heard only the beginning of what she said.

"Bequeathed, you might say," she answered. "They show the transition between Proust's first unfinished novel and the opening passage of *Remembrance of Things Past.* . . ." Gisèle wondered why her words seemed to fall like lead into the near-silence of the room, and why she was feeling gradually less and less at ease. It was as though she were digging her grave with every word.

"And" — he breathed out a long puff of blue smoke — "you have proof of what you're claiming here? You're in possession of these notebooks?"

Gisèle flustered. "I was in possession of them," she said. And she told him how she had given her bag to Émilienne, who had left it with the waiter at the Café de la

Gare, and why she had now to wait for Albert to return before she could get it back.

Professor Verdaillan got up out of his professorial chair, walked over to Gisèle, and, speaking in a paternal voice quite different from the tone he had used up until then, said, "Don't say another word about it, Gisèle, as long as you do not have these notebooks in hand. In the meantime, may I advise you strongly against publicizing what you have just told me in any way. The way I see it, you must at all costs — and I repeat for your own benefit, at all costs — keep this information to yourself and to yourself only. Let any word of this leak out and God only knows where it'll land you in this investigation of Mme Bertrand-Verdon's . . . um . . . death."

"Don't you think I should mention it to the police?" Gisèle asked, surprised and somewhat disconcerted by his vehemence.

"Absolutely not, Gisèle, absolutely not. Just think for a moment of the ideas that it might give them. . . . No, the best thing we can do now is to inquire at the Café de la Gare if this . . . Arthur? . . . Alfred?"

"Albert," she said softly.

"— if our man Albert has reappeared," he went on without a stumble. "Do you have a car?"

"No," Gisèle admitted. She looked at the floor and made another effort to get the discussion back onto the subject she was concerned about. "About my defense . . ."

"Don't worry about your defense," Professor Verdaillan assured her, a hint of impatience in his voice. "Give me your final version and we'll find a date that will suit . . . um . . . everybody. Right now, we have to get those notebooks back."

"I really don't want to impose on you —," Gisèle

began. She had the firm intention of going to the Café de la Gare by herself.

"Not at all, not at all. I insist," Guillaume Verdaillan said loudly with a wide sweep of his right arm, causing the ash of his cigarette to fall off without his noticing onto the patterned carpet.

And that was how Gisèle wound up in her thesis director's high-powered car, which brought them in record time to the Café de la Gare.

"Oh! There you are at last," exclaimed the proprietress when she saw them come in. "Albert's mother just called. Albert had an accident on his moped last night. He's laid up for a week at least."

"Did you ask about the bag?" Gisèle asked, her heart beating furiously.

"You bet I did. But his mother didn't know anything about it. She was calling from a pay phone at Lamousse. How are we going to manage on a market day without Albert? And then there's the wedding tomorrow night —"

"Where's Lamousse?" Professor Verdaillan wanted to know.

"It's about fifteen miles away," the proprietress said. "But I should warn you that the Teissandier farm isn't exactly easy to find."

"With a good map you can find anything," the professor said didactically. "Along with a few directions. Tell us —"

Fifteen minutes later the professor and his graduate student were charging through the flat countryside of the Beauce. Gisèle didn't quite know what to make of all the attention she was getting, and she had a sinking feeling that this would end badly. She bore the bumps and swerves of her advisor's breakneck driving style in silence, but they were making her sick to her stomach, and she couldn't help letting out a little shriek when the speeding vehicle entered a dangerous intersection and came within a hair's breadth of crashing into a yellow bus, the driver of which rolled down his window to vent his personal — and scatological — opinion of Parisian drivers.

17

THE CHÂTEAU DE LA MOISANDERIE was an immense, two-winged structure with extraordinary adjoining grounds that included, to one side, the untamed landscape of a park *à l'anglaise* whose disarray in the summer must have been delightful and, to the other, the geometrically ordered paths and flowerbeds of a French-style garden. The main building dated from the seventeenth century, along with the brick dovecote and a chapel that housed a notable *Presentation of the Virgin* by a disciple of Philippe de Champaigne. The building had been partially destroyed by fire during the Revolution, when the owners had been forced to emigrate temporarily to America, and it had been restored in the years following 1830 by a distant relative of the current Louis de la Moisandière. Although none of the original furniture had survived, the paneling and the ceilings were sufficiently preserved to give a good idea of their earlier splendor.

Inspector Foucheroux and Detective Djemani were shown not to the "King's Hall," where Louis XIV is said to have spent the night, but to an unadorned and unheated antechamber. Two green velvet chairs stood on either side of a bulbous chest of drawers, and there were a few worn armchairs arranged in a kind of semicircle around a card table in front of the unlit fireplace. The two visitors were looking at an imposing portrait of Charles Amanieu de la Moisandière on the road to Holland when the descendant of the painting's subject appeared in the flesh. They could see a slight resemblance in the shape of his forehead, the confident gaze of his brown eyes, and the somewhat condescending turn of his mouth.

"Louis de la Moisandière," he announced abruptly by way of greeting. "I imagine you are here to speak to M. de Chareilles about this unfortunate affair."

"That's right," Inspector Foucheroux said in a voice that revealed not the slightest emotion. "Detective Djemani and I would like to ask him a few questions about what he may have seen yesterday."

The lord of the Château de la Moisanderie let the question hang in the air for a moment before responding. "If you would just have a seat for a moment, I'll let him know you're here. I don't imagine you would object to his speaking to you in the presence of an attorney."

"But not in the least," Foucheroux assured him, adding, "although this is not at all an official visit. We're just trying to reconstruct the whereabouts of the victim during the day. M. de Chareilles will be a great help to us as a witness, since he was an intimate friend of Mme Bertrand-Verdon."

Charles-Louis de la Moisandière, seemingly on the point of putting an end to the little conversation, suddenly thought better of it. "I must warn you, Inspector, that M. de Chareilles is very upset by what has happened," he said brusquely. "I would advise you to choose your words carefully. Anything resembling an interrogation is out of the question."

It was obvious to Foucheroux that the head of the house was trying gallantly to protect the interests of his guest while repressing his all-too-obvious hostility toward the lawful agents of democracy. "You have my assurance that we will ask only what we have to ask, and that we will be very considerate of his grief," he said reassuringly.

His host stood for a moment fiddling nervously with his watch chain. "And you shouldn't take these rumors about a betrothal too seriously," he said finally. "True enough, Edward was thinking he might want to remarry at some point — after all, it's been over ten years since Blanche passed away — but countless things stood in the way of his ever actually formalizing an engagement with someone like Mme Bertrand-Verdon. . . . Whatever you may have heard, Inspector, I can assure you that no decision had been made. Why, just yesterday . . ." He paused for a moment. "But it's doubtless best that Edward explain all of that himself." Then, suddenly changing the subject, he asked, "I don't mean to be indiscreet, Inspector, but may I ask if you are related to the Clairmonteils, as my wife seems to think?"

Leila saw Foucheroux stiffen and his face go dark. "In a manner of speaking," he answered in a glacially polite tone.

Realizing that it was useless to pursue the issue — something that his good upbringing would have prevented him from doing in any event — M. de la Moisandière gave the inspector a look the meaning of which was transparent to everyone, turned on his heels, and left them with a curt, "I'll see if M. de Chareilles is ready to see you."

Alone again with Foucheroux, Leila had sense enough to keep quiet. She walked over to one of the large windows looking out onto a stone fountain, from which she could see a slender stream of water shooting upward into the air, and stood contemplating the carefully pruned boxwood trees and the skeletonlike trellises with their wiry arches that would disappear, come summer, behind the vines of a lush mauve wisteria.

"I don't appreciate their treating us like servants, Detective," her superior said suddenly. "Please excuse the haughtiness of the place. It's hereditary."

"That doesn't make any difference at all," she told him softly. "Really, it doesn't matter in the least."

But it mattered to him. He would never get used to his father-in-law having so many clones, all speaking with the same tone of voice, the same syntax, and the same haughty contempt, poorly concealed behind an exaggerated politeness. He had to get hold of himself. He couldn't allow his personal feelings and sensitivities to play a role. This Viscount of Chareilles should be heard objectively and without prejudice. He should be given the benefit of the doubt, every citizen's basic right.

A servant appeared and showed them to a delightful little rococo room where, standing in front of a Venetian secretary, M. de Chareilles, flanked by his host and his lawyer, was trying valiantly to look relaxed.

"Then we'll leave you to take care of the inspector yourself, Edward?" M. de la Moisandière asked his guest.

"If that's all right with you —"

"Of course it is, my dear friend, of course it is. You know where to find us if we can help." And he walked out along with the third gentleman, whom he introduced tersely in passing with a brief "Maître Laucournet."

By anyone's account, the Viscount of Chareilles was still a handsome man. Elegantly dressed, tall, slender, with an upright posture and a keen eye, he was the epitome of

149

what was commonly referred to as "old France." The tiny blue veins on his aristocratic hands and his ivory white hair were the only visible signs that he might in fact be older than he seemed. But it was his voice, the crackling, feeble quaver of an old man, that really gave away his age. "Please sit down, Inspector, Detective. . . . Since I'm told this is to be an informal little talk —"

"That's exactly right, M. de Chareilles. Detective Djemani and I would appreciate your giving us a minute or two of your time." Leila couldn't make out whether there was a note of irony in the inspector's voice or not. "We're sorry to disturb you this way," Foucheroux went on as he took a seat in one of the padded chairs with a gracefully rounded back, "but we're trying to retrace the movements of Mme Bertrand-Verdon, and we think you can help."

"Oh I understand, Inspector, I understand," the viscount said. "You're doing what you have to do. Let's get through this as quickly as possible. . . . I saw Adeline twice yesterday. Once in the early afternoon at Aunt Léonie's, and again at the dinner for the board of directors, at the Old Mill Inn."

"And what was she doing at Aunt Léonie's?"

"A dozen different things, as usual. She was a very busy young woman. I met her there at about two o'clock, just after she got in from Paris. I had arrived here at the Moisanderie two days earlier, and there was something we had to talk about —" He broke off suddenly. "We didn't talk long, because Adeline was furious with her secretary."

"Do you know why?" Inspector Foucheroux asked, knowing without having to check that Leila, who had sat down to his left, was writing everything down word for word.

"Something about some keys, I think. I must confess I

didn't really pay much attention. We had a decision to make. . . . We were wondering if we should announce . . ."

"Your marriage plans," the inspector helped him along.

"Oh! You already know about it, then," said M. de Chareilles wearily. "It was more a question of our engagement. Adeline was younger than I, less willing to wait. But she was very accomplished, very likable, and so dynamic. And she came from a good family. She was a direct descendant of Victoria Richelet Verdon, who had apparently wed a Charleville. I learned from Adeline that this Victoria was the grandmother of a nineteenth-century woman writer who lived in Louisiana and is best known as the author of a short novel that was something of a success at the turn of the century. Kate Chopin, do you know her?"

"*The Awakening*, yes, I've read it," the inspector answered mechanically. Even as he spoke, Clotilde's melodious voice echoed in his memory: "Don't tell me you've never heard of Kate Chopin! That's terrible! She wrote what you might call an American version of *Madame Bovary*, a real masterpiece. The ending is fabulous. You really should read it." And he had read it. Leila, fully aware of the unconscious associations to which her superior had fallen prey, waited patiently for him to regain control of the conversation. "Verdon . . . Where does the name come from exactly?" the inspector asked, deciding to play along.

"Well, there are the canyons of the river that bears that name in Castellane-Gréoulx, of course, but in this case we would have to trace the name to Verdon-sur-Mer, in the Gironde. That was on her mother's side. On her father's side, the Bertrands, we're obviously talking about something else altogether." Dumbfounded, Leila had a hard time concealing her growing astonishment as the viscount went on. "There was no relation to Bertrand of Born, the troubadour, nor, thank heavens, to the general of that name under Napoleon, but rather to the mathematician Joseph and his son, Marcel-Alexandre. Adeline used a double name to honor the memory of her mother, as well as to flaunt a slight feminist tendency of hers. She always liked to stir things up a little. . . . At any rate, she was thinking about founding another literary society, the Kate Chopin Association, over which she would have presided. She had so many projects. . . ."

Leila couldn't help being reminded of Tinkerbell, the fairy in *Peter Pan* who scatters stardust on children's eyes from the tip of her wand. It was as though Adeline Bertrand-Verdon had thrown dust into the eyes of this man, who was certainly no fool, who was knowledgeable, who had dignity. . . .

"I truly loved Adeline," he concluded with obvious sincerity. "Her death grieves me beyond words."

Foucheroux cast about for a response that would hurt the elderly gentleman as little as possible. "We sympathize with your loss, M. de Chareilles. I trust that you will do all that is in your power to help us find the person who is responsible for her death."

"I still can't believe it. . . . She had a penchant for puns, for familiar quotations. . . . Just yesterday evening, she was in such good spirits. . . ."

"That's the last time you saw her?"

"The last time, yes," he sighed. "I left her at the foot of the stairs, when they told me that M. de la Moisandière's chauffeur was waiting for me at the door. . . . At around ten o'clock."

"You were the first to leave, then?" asked the inspector softly with a knowing glance at his detective.

"Yes, I believe so, since the other members of the board and M. Rainsford were staying at the hotel."

"And do you know whether Mme Bertrand-Verdon was intending to meet anyone later that evening?"

"Oh no, I'm certain she had no such intention at all, Inspector. She herself told me she didn't want to be disturbed, since there were still a number of details she had to take care of before the convention." *Didn't want to be disturbed* — the same phrase exactly they had heard from Philippe Desforge! Inspector Foucheroux heard Leila shift slightly on her fluted chair and guessed that she had made the same connection. "Adeline never lied," the Viscount of Chareilles stated firmly.

Overcoming his strong aversion to what he was about to do, Foucheroux turned to face Leila. "Detective?" he said simply. She knew immediately what he expected from her.

"It seems there has been a misunderstanding on a couple of points," she said evenly. "The name Bertrand, for one. Adeline Bertrand's maiden name was Verdon —"

The viscount gave her a puzzled look. "Verdon was the name of her mother and Bertrand that of her father, as I explained to you. That's what she always gave me to understand."

"That's not quite correct," Leila said, choosing her words as tactfully as she could, but there was no avoiding the truth. "Verdon was her maiden name," she said simply. "Bertrand was the name of her husband."

"Her husband? She was a widow?"

"No." Foucheroux spoke with a note of regret.

"You don't mean . . . She wasn't . . ." He was incapable of going any further.

"I'm afraid so. She was divorced."

"But that's not possible," the viscount objected loudly.

153

"Or the marriage was annulled. She knew perfectly well . . . She would never have . . ."

"I'm afraid so," Foucheroux said again. "The marriage took place in Nemours, at the Sainte-Marie-des-Champs church. We have a copy of the act of divorce. . . . Detective Djemani —" He glanced at Leila.

"It's no use," the viscount said feebly and got up out of his chair before she could make the slightest move toward her bag. "I don't want to see it. If you will excuse me, please —" He staggered toward the door, two red spots glowing on his pale cheeks, a nervous tic twisting the left corner of his tightly pressed lips into a grotesque spasm. On his way out, he inadvertently dropped a small silk handkerchief that matched his tie onto the floor.

"He didn't know," Foucheroux said as soon as the viscount was gone, carefully picking up the square patch of fabric.

"And so he had no motive," Leila concluded for him.

"Nor did he have the opportunity, if indeed the chauffeur brought him straight back here and if there are witnesses who can testify that he didn't go out again —"

"Unless we're dealing with another acting genius, but —" She was interrupted by the sudden entrance of M. de la Moisandière.

"Congratulations, Inspector," he bellowed. "Thanks to you, the Viscount of Chareilles, who has heart trouble, is having a fit. When they hear about your indescribable methods, I'm sure your superiors will be most impressed indeed by the way you and your detective conduct your investigations. May I ask you —"

"We were just about to leave," Foucheroux cut in calmly. "If you would let us know when M. de Chareilles's physical and mental state is sufficiently recovered to sign his deposition, we will send an agent from the Criminal

Investigation Department to draw up the report. And we can find our own way out, thank you. Detective Djemani —"

Leila Djemani had closed her notebook and was already on her feet. With a toneless "Good day" and a respectful nod of the head, she stepped past M. de la Moisandière and fell in behind Inspector Foucheroux, who was already walking off in long, awkward strides, his face set in an impenetrable expression. He didn't utter a word in the car on the way back, muttering only a terse "could be" when Leila exclaimed that the sports car ahead of them, which had just sped by a stop sign, looked a lot like Professor Verdaillan's Renault.

"To the police station," he ordered as soon as they were in sight of the village.

18

LOCATING THE TEISSANDIER FARM was a difficult task indeed, in spite of the map and the café proprietress's copious directions. After twice finding himself back at the state highway, Professor Verdaillan turned down a narrower road, driving so fast that Gisèle could scarcely make out the route number on the signposts. Then, claiming he knew just where they were, he turned onto an even smaller road that led them to the edge of a grayish pond, around which clusters of doleful carrion crows, perched in the branches of some naked poplars, croaked a noisy protest against the intruders.

With a kick to the accelerator that caused a minor avalanche, Guillaume Verdaillan wheeled around and raced back the way they had come, then turned north onto another little road strikingly similar to the one they had just left, which came to an equally unequivocal dead end in front of an abandoned shed. A sign on the door, which was swinging open and shut in the wind, proudly announced: Private Property. No Trespassing.

"Where in the hell are we?" he railed. "A map is no use at all if it doesn't tell you how to tell one road from another!"

Gisèle's sense of direction was not flawless, but she was somewhat familiar with the region, and she suggested that they get back onto the state highway and turn off at the second intersection, the one marked with a cross on the little hand-drawn map they were using as a guide. After going in circles for the better part of an hour — quite a feat in a part of the country where everything is cut up into squares and rectangles — they finally arrived at a three-way intersection with an old wooden sign that pointed the way to Lamousse. "We're here," Gisèle said timidly, and pointed at a blue cross on the paper lying unfolded on her lap.

"We are, are we?" the professor said skeptically, and, with a roar of the engine that shook the branches of a sparse thicket, he charged toward one of the isolated houses, whose bright red roof reminded Gisèle of the little plastic hotels that are bought and sold in the game of Monopoly.

The farm itself was composed of two separate cob-wall buildings and an immense silo. As they got out of the car, a Flemish sheepdog chained to a post started to bark ferociously, and the front door of the main building swung open to reveal a little girl with unkempt pigtails, wearing a blue apron. "Pipe down, Chani, you'll wake Albert up," she shouted authoritatively. In a glance she took in the young woman's fine leather shoes and her companion's striped suit. "You're from town," she announced in the almost comically stern voice of a child who feels called on to assume the responsibilities of an adult.

"From Paris," Professor Verdaillan corrected her without the least hint of a smile. "Is this the Teissandier farm?"

"Yes," she said. "Are you from the insurance company?"

157

"What? Uh . . . no!" said Guillaume Verdaillan, rather taken aback by the little girl's self-assurance. "We're here . . . We'd like to talk to Albert."

"My brother's not home," the child asserted, casting an oblique glance at the ground and tugging at a corner of her apron.

"But you just told the dog —" The professor realized suddenly the absurdity of what he was about to say and broke off.

Gisèle decided to intercede. "What's your name?" she asked in her kindest voice.

"Elodia."

"That's a nice name. It reminds me of music. Are your parents home, Elodia?"

The little girl paused for a moment before shaking her head. "They're in Courville," she said. Then, as though she were reciting a line she had learned by heart, she added hurriedly: "They'll be back in just a moment."

"And you're not in school today?" Gisèle asked with a smile.

"It's because I had the mumps," the child explained. Professor Verdaillan took a step back. "And last night I had an asthma attack because —"

"It is extremely important that we speak to Albert," the professor broke in sternly, having lost all patience with this useless prattle and feeling less than inclined to listen to a comprehensive catalog of the Teissandier family's childhood illnesses. "May we come in?"

Elodia's face went dark as a storm, and she would doubtless have run into the house and locked the door if Gisèle had not had the presence of mind to trot out the oldest temptation in the book. "Do you want a piece of candy?" she asked, pulling a box of acid drops from her purse and opening the gold-colored lid.

"Usually I like Pine Brothers better," the little girl announced as she wavered between two red ones, unable to decide if they were cherry or raspberry, before finally stretching out an ink-stained finger for what she hoped was a mint-flavored green one.

Gisèle was touched by the child's show of restraint in this conflict of love and duty. "You can have the whole box," she said. Her generosity earned her a "Thank you" and a broad smile, followed by an abrupt "You can come in now."

Scarcely believing his ears and a bit irked at the ease of his student's victory, Professor Verdaillan started toward the door. "You should have majored in child psychology, Mlle Dambert," he muttered under his breath. But the girl stopped him in midstride.

"Not you. The lady." Her voice left no room for argument. Professor Verdaillan was perceptive enough to recognize the unshakable stubbornness of an offended child.

"I'll be in the car," he flung at Gisèle. "Come and get me when —"

"Of course," the young woman answered rather too promptly as she followed Elodia through the door.

The bright and spacious room Gisèle walked into was clearly the heart of the house. The rays of the sun filtered in through two rows of potted geraniums sitting in unseasonably late bloom on the windowsills. An enormous oak table occupied the middle of the room, surrounded by eight straw-bottomed chairs. The old sink was embellished by a border of blue-and-white-glazed tiles, and the drabness of the kitchen appliances disappeared in the radiant glow of a fire that was crackling cheerily in the enormous stone fireplace. Everything seemed imbued with a friendly smell of warm bread, and Gisèle accepted without

159

a moment's hesitation when Elodia asked if she would like a cup of coffee.

The girl went over to an enormous cupboard, took down a mug and a tin box of sugar lumps, got a spoon out of the drawer, and placed everything carefully onto the table. Then she took up a spuming coffeepot and, with a look of great concentration on her face, filled the cup to the rim.

"Thank you, Elodia," said Gisèle. "We should leave enough for Albert, shouldn't we?" she asked, smiling conspiratorially.

Elodia returned her smile. "He's asleep," she whispered. "I'm protecting him."

Gisèle wondered what the danger was, but asked only, "Is he sick?"

"He had an accident," Elodia explained, knitting her delicate brows. Her brown eyes reminded Gisèle of those of a squirrel. "My mother gave him a special tea to make him fall asleep." Just then, Gisèle happened to cast her eye on the drawing that Elodia would probably have finished by now if she hadn't gotten up to discover the cause of Chani's frenzied barking. It showed a masked man, dressed all in black, standing at the center of a web of bright yellow lights and brandishing a long dagger above the face of a second man lying on the ground at his feet. The upturned wheels of a red bicycle could be seen in the background, below a thin sliver of moon and two little stars. Gisèle had a sudden intuition, and in a flash she knew just what had happened.

"You're good at drawing, Elodia," she said, hiding her consternation. She pointed at the figure on the ground. "Is that Albert?"

"Yeah," the little girl admitted. "But it's a secret. He's

afraid the man in black is going to kill him. I heard him telling Christian the whole story last night."

"Christian?"

"My other brother, who works in Chartres," she said, clearly thinking this was all the explanation that was needed. She added a few extra stars to her drawing with a silver crayon.

Suddenly terrified, Gisèle felt the blood drain from her face. The wildest thoughts shot through her mind, and she had to struggle to stay calm in front of Elodia, who was again gazing up at her with a look of utter confidence. She forced herself to smile, wanting above all not to poison this earnest little creature with even the least part of her fears. Clearly, the girl had a gift for drawing: the composition, the choice of colors, the candidness of the pastiche testified incontrovertibly to the wit and the talent of the painter. Like all the great artists, Elodia had succeeded in rendering, in her own way, another person's experience. The terror her brother must have felt in the moment he was attacked, vividly captured in a few strokes of the crayon, seemed to jump up off the page as though by magic.

Gisèle didn't doubt for a moment that the incident had something to do with the loss of the notebooks, and with a jolt she realized that the notebooks themselves were connected to Adeline Bertrand-Verdon's murder. The attacker was a composite of Zorro, Batman, and Darth Vader, transformed by the imagination of Albert's little sister into a single fiend. Suddenly, inexplicably, the face of Guillaume Verdaillan seemed to appear behind the mask. When she thought about it, he hadn't seemed overly surprised when she had told him about the 1905 notebooks, and the way he had insisted on accompanying her afterward to the Café de la Gare was more than a little odd. Just like the way he had gotten "lost" on the little country roads . . . as though to make a show of the fact that he didn't know the way to the Teissandier farm. Gisèle reeled at the thought. If it was true, then all three of them were in imminent danger — Elodia, Albert, and herself.

"Are you tired?" Elodia inquired in her clear little voice. Just then, they heard three loud knocks at the door.

"Don't answer," Gisèle commanded instinctively. "Let's go see Albert. Quick —" There was something urgent in her voice that made Elodia obey without a word. They left the warmth of the kitchen and went into a long hallway with several doors at the far end. Elodia knocked at the last of them.

"Albert! Albert!" she called out urgently. Hearing no response, she turned the knob and the door swung open to reveal the chaotic clutter of a typical adolescent's bedroom, adorned with posters portraying a balanced mix of rock stars and pinups posing provocatively in tiny bikinis. There was a pervasive smell of sneakers. The bed, unmade, was empty, and the only window in the room stood open. Albert had leapt to freedom.

"Oh!" was all Elodia could say. She grabbed Gisèle's hand. "He's gone!"

Gisèle gave the little girl a puzzled look and was about to ask if she had any idea where he could have gone when they heard, muffled but perfectly identifiable, the characteristic crack of a gunshot. In a flash Elodia freed her hand from Gisèle's, eluded her desperate attempt to hold her back, and ran outside in a panic, screaming "Albert! Albert!"

The two of them arrived simultaneously in the front yard, where they were treated to what looked like a scene from some tragicomic theater play. Looking every bit like a rabid beast, Chani was straining at his chain and barking up a storm while Guillaume Verdaillan, bent over the front left fender of his car with his hands above his head, was having a dialogue of the deaf with a livid redheaded youth who was aiming a hunting rifle straight at his chest.

"Thought you could sneak up on me twice, huh?" the boy was screaming.

"Twice?" the professor hurled back, trying desperately to make himself heard above the barking of the dog. "Twice? What do you mean? I've never seen you before!"

"Oh, you've never seen me before, have you?" Albert sneered. He saw Elodia and Gisèle in the doorway. "Come here, Lodie," he called out anxiously. Torn between conflicting emotions and terrified by the sight of her brother's fury, Elodia glanced from Gisèle to Guillaume Verdaillan to her brother, then back to Gisèle before bursting suddenly into tears, overwhelmed by the situation.

"Don't be afraid, Lodie. Come here," Albert said again. "And you," he screamed at Gisèle, "go stand next to him." He pointed his rifle at Professor Verdaillan.

Gisèle gave Elodia's shoulder a gentle squeeze and nudged her forward. "Do what your brother tells you," she said with a little smile and went to stand next to Guillaume Verdaillan, who told her bluntly that they were at the mercy of a lunatic.

"The kid's crazy! Stark raving mad!" he mumbled into his beard.

"I don't think so," whispered Gisèle.

"How do you explain —"

"Enough chitchat," Albert shouted, relieved to see his sister standing safely at his side. "I want to know how you found me and what you were doing snooping around here."

163

"It's all my fault," Gisèle hurried to explain. "It's because of my bag —"

"Aha! The same bag that almost got me killed last night by this big oaf!" He gestured with the muzzle of his rifle at Guillaume Verdaillan. "What's in your bag, anyway, is it full of gold?" The so-called oaf didn't make a sound. Gisèle shook her head.

"Albert —," Elodia started to say softly.

"And to think that I took the damn bag to do Émilienne a favor," the youth shouted in disgust. "It's against the boss's rules to keep things for the clients anyway!"

"That's just it, it was your boss who told us how to find you," Gisèle set in. "She drew us a map. I can show it to you. It's in the car."

"Don't move!" Albert shouted, his finger still on the trigger. "Lodie, go and see," he said to his sister. The little girl obeyed, ran around the Renault, and saw, lying on the front seat, the sheet of letterhead from the Hôtel de Guermantes with a crude map of the area.

"It's true, Albert," she called out. And softly, to Gisèle: "Don't worry, he's not mean."

"I'm sorry to have caused so much trouble," Gisèle began, "but it's all an accident. There are some documents in the bag that are very important for my work, and you are the only —"

"Then I suggest you go look for them in Italy," the youth broke in.

"In Italy?" Gisèle and the professor said in unison.

Convinced that their surprise at what he had said might be genuine, Albert lowered his rifle just enough to explain — exactly as he had the night before, except that this time he had the upper hand — what had probably happened to the bag in question. As he spoke, Professor

Verdaillan began to relax and his spirits seemed noticeably to improve, whereas Gisèle grew more and more tense. When the young man got to the end, she had an uncontrollable nervous reaction and, like Elodia a moment before, she burst into tears. "Crybaby!" Yvonne's malicious voice murmured in the wind. "Crybaby!"

"Albert, look what you've done now," said Elodia angrily. In the distance, they heard the rumble of an approaching vehicle.

"Scram!" the young man commanded brusquely. "And don't let me see you around here again!"

"We could sue, you know," grumbled Professor Verdaillan just loud enough to be heard as soon as he was safely seated behind the wheel of his car.

"Wait a minute!" Elodia pleaded. Quick as an arrow, she flew through the open kitchen door and reappeared two seconds later with a scrap of paper in her hand. With a broad, satisfied smile, she handed her drawing to Gisèle, who had opened the window on her side of the car. "A going-away present —"

*

When the neighbors came up to find out what had happened, Albert explained calmly that he had fired into the air to scare off a band of crows. And when they joked curiously about the momentous occasion that had prompted a visit from Paris, he said simply, "The Parisians can all rot in hell, as far as I'm concerned." Chani yelped in approval before going back to his shed, wagging his tail in contentment at the three "good dog's" and the vigorous pats on the head that he garnered from his master, who was generally not one for extravagant displays of affection.

*

In the car on the way back, Gisèle didn't say a word. She scarcely noticed the old truck they passed on the way out, the stop sign Verdaillan ran, the little tune he hummed unconsciously, nervously, his lips pressed tightly together, feigning the stoic detachment of a man who has withstood a challenge. She could think of nothing but the notebooks that were lost again, this time for good, no doubt. . . . And of what that meant.

So it took her completely by surprise when Guillaume Verdaillan braked precipitously, turned onto a little dirt road, and came to a sudden stop in the middle of a large deserted field. He lit a cigarette and, turning to face Gisèle, declared bluntly, "So, Mlle Dambert, it's time you and I had a little chat."

19

INSPECTOR FOUCHEROUX and Detective Djemani walked into the police station and found Bernard Tournadre seated at his desk, a telephone receiver cradled on his left shoulder, scribbling furiously on a notepad. He looked up. "Ah, here he is right now," he said with a sigh of relief. He motioned Foucheroux over to the desk. "The lab —"

An official-sounding voice summed up for the inspector's benefit the preliminary results of the autopsy. The time of death was approximately eleven P.M. the previous day. It had ensued instantly and had been caused by a single blow to the right temple of a blunt plaster object, dealt with great force by an assailant as tall or taller than the victim. There were also traces of a strong dose of soporific — Halcion, probably — along with a mix of anti-depressants and a relatively high alcohol count. There were traces of desquamation along the right side of the neck and on the left wrist. Otherwise they had found nothing out of the ordinary, except for evidence of an aborted pregnancy and of an appendectomy that had been carried out some twenty years earlier. Her blood type was O. "If there are no other questions, we'll go ahead and send off the report," the voice on the other end concluded.

"That will be fine, thank you," answered Foucheroux. He hung up and turned to Officer Tournadre. "Meynadier's preliminary suppositions turned out to be accurate. May I present Detective Djemani —" Purposefully ignoring the look of surprise that flashed for a moment in Bernard Tournadre's eyes, Leila amicably held out her hand to the sergeant as her superior started to go over their immediate agenda. "I asked Gisèle Dambert to meet us here at one, and Professor Verdaillan will be coming in as well to sign his statement. May I call on your staff to draft the depositions?"

"Of course, Inspector. Duval is at your disposal. He's the best typist around here. As you can see, our equipment is not exactly ultramodern," the sergeant said jokingly, with a rueful glance at a manual typewriter in the corner.

Just then Professor Rainsford burst into the office, brandishing a scrap of blue paper. "Aha! Inspector! I've found you at last!" he said reproachfully, catching his breath. "I just got a telegram from my brother. I have to return to the States immediately. An imminent death in the family —"

"I'm terribly sorry," Foucheroux said politely as he glanced at the brief message held out to him: "Granny dying. Come home immediately. Bob."

"Has your grandmother been ill for some time?"

"She had a stroke a few months ago, and I'm very worried about her, Inspector. Her condition must have gotten worse, as I feared —"

"You're probably right," the inspector conceded. "I see

168

no reason we can't let you leave the country tomorrow, or the day after at the latest."

"Tomorrow or the day after!" the professor sputtered. "But I was going to return to Paris immediately and take the first plane to Boston! I reserved a seat on the 6:30 flight!"

"I'm sorry, but you'll have to cancel, M. Rainsford. As a witness you're involved in a criminal investigation, and you are required to stay in the vicinity. In fact, I need your sworn statement as soon as we're ready to draft it. Would five o'clock suit you —"

"What would suit me is to call my embassy!" shouted Rainsford, suddenly livid with anger. Shifting into his native tongue, he protested vociferously against this violation of his "civil rights."

"But you're perfectly free to call whomever you please. There's a phone booth two blocks down on your right," the imperturbable Foucheroux said cheerfully.

Sergeant Tournadre gave a low whistle of reproach as soon as the professor had left. "Now there's an American who's lost all trace of Britain's famous art of understatement!"

"Do you think the murder was committed in a state of momentary insanity?" Leila asked.

"By a psychotic?" Tournadre joined in.

"Possibly. Considering the circumstances, it doesn't seem to have been a premeditated crime," reasoned Foucheroux. "As for the psychosis, the only sign we've seen of something like that is an acute case of what Freud calls 'family romance' — and apparently the victim was the only one affected. The most important thing now is to find the weapon." He looked at his watch. "I'm almost inclined to go directly to Aunt Léonie's. Detective Djemani?" Leila nodded her agreement, and the two of them set off, leaving instructions on the way out for Gisèle Dambert to wait in the event that they were a little late getting back.

When they got to Aunt Léonie's house, they were greeted in the corridor by the angry voices of an older woman and a pimply adolescent boy in the midst of a heated argument. "It's like I said, Émilienne," the boy was saying. "I brought it in the day before yesterday."

"Don't you lie to me, Théodore," the woman scolded. "I found it outside yesterday morning when I got here. Stop trying to tell me I don't know what I saw with my own eyes!"

"Maybe it was outside yesterday morning, but I took it inside the night before, just like you said," Théodore persisted. "I even asked the secretary where to put it, and she made me carry it upstairs to the office."

"To the office! Now that's a new one! We never keep it in the office. We —" Émilienne broke off in midsentence when she saw the two strangers trespassing on her territory. "If you're here for the tour, you're too early," she said sharply. "Come back at two-thirty."

"We're not here for the tour," the tall, slender gentleman corrected her. "I'm Inspector Foucheroux, and this is Detective Djemani. You must be Émilienne Robichoux. You're the one who discovered —"

But Émilienne, who had recovered her presence of mind, was not inclined to be reminded so abruptly of her "gruesome discovery." "I already made my statement at the police station," she declared indignantly, gaping in open astonishment at the kind of person the police were recruiting for their detective squad nowadays.

"I read it with my utmost attention, Mme Robichoux," the inspector said reassuringly, "and there are just a few other points I thought you could help us with."

170

"Well, it's not exactly a convenient time," Émilienne answered, somewhat mollified. "Considering that I have to get the whole ground floor ready for the tour — and that the youth of today is less than reliable," she added, with a vindictive glance in Théodore's direction.

"If there's nothing else you need me to do —," the latter began.

"Nothing else I need you to do!" howled Émilienne. "With my back acting up! I need you to bring the statue in, how many times do I have to tell you! But not now," she said regretfully. "After the tour. Come back at five."

And the young man, happy to get off so lightly, scurried off with a timorous "Bye, folks."

Émilienne rolled her eyes. "Youth," she sighed with a shrug of her shoulders. "Allergic to work, all of them. In my day —" But suddenly remembering that she was in the presence of two officers of the law, she decided against enumerating the various sources of undeclared income that had so occupied her early years. "Where do you want to sit?" she asked unceremoniously. "In the visitor center?"

"Why not?" Foucheroux agreed and fell into step behind the caretaker, who had not waited for his answer to push open the door to a dreary room with two bookshelves piled high with translations of Proust's works in all the languages of the globe. In the middle of the room stood a large table that served double duty as a cashier's stand and a display case and was covered with foldouts, sample postcards, and color photographs of the writer as a child, as a young man, and on his deathbed. A discreet sign announced the price of admission, and a stack of membership applications was positioned prominently at the front of the table in hopes of transforming the occasional visitor into a permanent adherent of the Proust Association. On the wall a print of Vermeer's *View of Delft* had been affixed next to a contemporary interpretation of *Remembrance of Things Past* by a painter whose name was indecipherable and was likely to remain so for all eternity. By contrast, a series of admirable black-and-white photographs of the places figuring in Proust's masterpiece, signed "F-X B.," gave an accurate idea of what an inspired artist could do with the same subject. "Another universe," Foucheroux said to himself, remembering something his sister Marylis had told him.

"Could you tell us, madame, when you last saw the president?" Foucheroux asked, returning to the reality at hand.

"Last *saw*," Émilienne said again. "You mean before . . . you mean alive. . . . May I sit down?" she said finally as she lowered herself onto one of the six uninviting chairs lined up against the wall.

"Please do. Why don't we all take a seat?" he said, motioning discreetly to Leila and pulling up another chair for himself.

"I can't really say I saw her the day before yesterday," Émilienne began, recovering her talkative self as soon as they were all seated in a little circle. "I came by in the afternoon to ask the secretary to sign my overtime statement. There'd been tons of extra work, what with the weather and all the visitors. . . . I didn't see Mme Bertrand-Verdon, but I heard her. . . ." She hesitated. "I didn't see Mlle Dambert either, but I heard them both. . . . Not that I was trying to spy on them or anything. It was just that . . . they were having an argument."

"An argument," Foucheroux said flatly, showing no particular interest and looking a little as though he doubted her claim. Leila, recognizing one of her superior's favorite strategies, waited with bated breath for Émilienne to defend her credibility.

172

"I'm not in the habit of eavesdropping," she said hotly, "but they were talking so loudly that you'd have to be deaf not to have heard them. When I got here, Mlle Dambert was sobbing. 'You're a thief!' she said over and over."

"'You're a thief,' those were her exact words?"

"Yes, that's exactly what she said. And Mme Bertrand-Verdon was shouting at her that she would sue her for lee . . . lie . . ."

"Libel?" Leila guessed.

"Libel, yes, that's what she said," Émilienne went on, undeterred by her momentary lapse. "And then she said, 'Listen, my dear, it'll be your word against mine, and who do you think people are going to believe?' And Mlle Dambert said that no one could talk from beyond the grave, and — Oh!" Émilienne clapped her hand to her mouth, suddenly realizing what her words might imply. "I don't mean . . . I don't think . . . I'm just repeating what I heard," she managed finally. "And I don't know what happened after that, because I decided it wasn't the best moment to ask them about my overtime, and that's when I left."

"What you've just told us is of the utmost importance," Foucheroux said gravely. "You may have to testify —"

"Oh no," Émilienne protested, suddenly panicking at the thought of the courtroom. "I don't want to get anybody in trouble. I —"

"We understand completely how you feel, and I'm grateful for your help. We won't call on you unless it's absolutely necessary. Detective Djemani is just going to ask you to sign a piece of paper so that you don't have to go back to the police station. Anything else, Detective?"

"No, not really," said Leila, taking her cue. "If I could ask you to sign here," she said to Émilienne with a smile, "after you've read —"

"I don't have my glasses," Émilienne broke in, looking for a way out.

"If it's your reading glasses you need, I happen to have a pair in my purse," Leila said amicably. "Would you like to use them?"

"Well . . . I can give it a try, I suppose," Émilienne mumbled. And taking the little spectacles Leila held out to her, she pretended to struggle line by line through the statement Leila had drawn up, sniffed once or twice, nodded, and signed.

"Thank you," said Foucheroux. "And now we'll let you get on with your work, won't we, Detective?"

"That's right," Leila concurred. And on a sudden impulse: "Would you like us to help you with the statue you were talking about?"

"Oh, no thanks. Théodore will be back at five. And this time he really will bring it in, and not up to the office, you can be sure of that, what with the plaster flaking off all over the place —" Jean-Pierre Foucheroux and Leila Djemani gave each other a look that went from disbelief to hope to sudden jubilation.

"And," he asked haltingly, "where is this statue?"

"Well . . . in its place, of course, in the middle of the garden, because Théodore didn't put it inside. He said he did, but he's lying through his teeth! You can go and see it, if you like. I've got work to do," Émilienne said. And with that, she rose from her chair, putting the interview to an end.

A moment later, Inspector Foucheroux and Detective Djemani were standing in the garden, looking intently at the charming little plaster reproduction of a bathing girl that had been sculpted by one of the great artists of the eighteenth century. They wasted no time admiring the girl's graciously angled knee, the elegant curve of her shoulders, or the sphinxlike smile on her delicately curved lips. They saw nothing but a cluster of tiny brownish spots on her bare feet that convinced them instantly that they had found the murder weapon. "We have to get this to the lab, immediately," murmured Foucheroux.

"And get everybody's fingerprints within an hour, I guess?" sighed Detective Djemani.

"Good guess, Detective. Shall we get to work?"

A few minutes later, a dumbfounded Émilienne stood by as a team of three experts with rubber gloves painstakingly wrapped the little statue in a large white canvas. They left noiselessly, just as they had arrived, leaving an ugly little brown hole in the middle of the flower bed.

20

GISÈLE HAD BEEN SITTING for over half an hour in a small, windowless chamber with an old radiator that was doing little to dispel the chill. She wondered if the police were making her wait here in order to exacerbate her already acute state of anxiety and weaken her resistance. How much did they know? Who had talked? Which of her lies had they uncovered? Nervously, she braided and unbraided the fringe of her scarf. She had been forced to take so many risks all at once, confronted as she was with two separate crises that had somehow become inextricably entangled, all because of Yvonne. And how could she talk her way out, now that Professor Verdaillan had made her promise to keep quiet? She had to gain time. Gain time to rearrange the truth. Play dumb. Swear she had promised to help André Larivière conduct the tour that was to take place in less than an hour . . .

After the terrible fight with Adeline that had left her with no alternative but to commit a crime, Gisèle had sat in her office into the late afternoon, desperately planning her counteroffensive, when Yvonne had called. It was such a rare occurrence that for a moment Gisèle had no idea who it was.

"Hello?" the feeble voice on the other end of the line stammered, "Aunt Léonie's? May I speak with Mlle Gisèle Dambert, please?"

"This is she," she answered, puzzled.

"Oh, Gisèle, thank God you're there. . . . It's me, Yvonne." Her voice rose and fell with each syllable, as though she had lost all control over her exhausted vocal cords. "I have to talk to you, Gisèle —"

"Sure, Yvonne," Gisèle said, wresting control over her own state of near-hysteria and forcing herself to remain calm. "I'm all ears."

"No, not like this . . . You don't understand. I have to talk to you . . . for real," Yvonne pleaded like a little girl.

"What happened?" Gisèle asked, mustering all her patience.

"The most amazing thing . . . I'm so happy. . . . I'm so miserable. . . ." She was in a state of total incoherence. For several minutes, brief bursts of nonsensical speech followed long lapses of silence until finally, with a little gasp, she came out with it. "I'm going to leave Jacques."

"Yvonne! What about the children?" Gisèle cried indignantly before she could stop herself.

"That's just it, Gisèle, that's what I have to talk to you about. If you only knew . . ."

Gisèle thought for a moment, looked at her watch, and came up with a single solution. She suggested it to her sister reluctantly, expecting her to refuse. "You can come and meet me here, Yvonne. We'll drive back to Paris together. . . . I can come back here tomorrow morning. No one needs to know about it. It's just between you and me."

"I'll be there as soon as I can." She had not hesitated

177

for an instant. She who had never confided anything to Gisèle, who hated driving at night, who had a terrible sense of direction. "I'll find you," she decreed peremptorily. "Thanks, Gisèle. I knew I could count on you." Her voice was firmer now. "I'm coming."

And when she had finally arrived in all her blond-haired glory, looking enticingly fragile under the strain of her nervous tension, Yvonne had collapsed onto the only armchair in the office and coiled up her long, perennially smooth-skinned legs. And from the lips of her perfect mouth had emerged the most commonplace sentence in the language: "I'm in love." Little did she suspect that she was about to become an unwitting accomplice in an affair of a very different nature.

*

Gisèle straightened up abruptly as she heard steps just outside the door, which opened to reveal the slightly stooped figure of Jean-Pierre Foucheroux. He seemed as though he had something on his mind and peered at her with what she took to be outright suspicion. He really does look like Al Gore, she couldn't help thinking as she glanced obliquely at his brown hair neatly parted on the side, his straight nose, his square chin, the determined cut of his mouth. He's wearing the same tie he had on yesterday, she thought. And she looked intensely at the blue and red silk stripes, which went perfectly with his white shirt and his navy blue suit. Why didn't he say anything? And where was Leila Djemani? More than anything else in the world, Gisèle suddenly wished for the presence of this woman to whom she might actually be able to talk. . . .

As though in answer to her dreams, the door opened a second time and Detective Djemani came in, sat down

178

next to her superior, and waited wordlessly for him to begin. All the little scenarios that Gisèle had thought up about how Leila would come tacitly to her aid evaporated in thin air. The whole room began to reel before her eyes.

"Would you like some water?" Detective Djemani asked flatly.

Gisèle nodded. The door was opened, closed, and opened again, and a glass of water was placed on the table in front of her. She took a sip. Inspector Foucheroux had remained standing the whole time and still had not uttered a word. Unable to bear the silence, Gisèle forced herself to speak. "I promised M. Larivière that I would help him conduct the tour this afternoon. Could we perhaps postpone this until later? . . . Since it's almost two o'clock —" Contrary to her expectations, he didn't raise his eyebrows in a look of disapproval, didn't inform her sarcastically that the police were not at her disposal, didn't cite paragraph such-and-such of article so-and-so of the penal code, authorizing him to detain her as long as he deemed necessary for the purposes of his investigation. Worse, he didn't say anything at all. Not a muscle moved on his impassive face, nothing appeared in the gray eyes that were fixed upon her. . . . Leila Djemani seemed to have been struck dumb as well, although she did shift slightly on her chair, revealing a telltale little bulge under her left arm. I can't believe she has a gun, Gisèle thought stupidly. Snatches of newspaper articles and TV news reports shot through her mind, along with a barrage of technical terms: ".357 Magnum," "snub-nosed .38 special" . . . Mechanically, her selective memory churned out its string of associations while she struggled with all her might to dissociate what she wanted Leila to be — a secret ally, a friend, a sister — from what she was: a police detective.

"Everyone's going to be there. They'll need me,"

Gisèle heard her hoarse voice saying as she tried desperately to shield herself behind her professional duty.

"You're in luck, Mlle Dambert," Inspector Foucheroux said finally. "We need to be there for the tour ourselves, and we wouldn't want to keep you from carrying out your functions. We'll all go together at two-thirty. But first you have more than enough time to tell us what really happened yesterday, what the argument you had with Mme Bertrand-Verdon was about, and what you were doing in her room at nine-fifty in the evening." He paused. "Yes, Mlle Dambert?"

So there it was. It was almost a relief, if that was all they knew, if they hadn't heard about the theft of the manuscripts. Gisèle saw Leila open her notebook and realized there was no way out. She decided she would tell them as much as she could, dressing up the facts here and there to protect Yvonne.

"Mme Bertrand-Verdon and I had a . . . um . . . disagreement about the agenda for the convention. She wanted to announce certain changes. . . . She was planning on making some sort of staff reduction —"

"She was going to fire you?" Foucheroux asked bluntly.

"That was one of the options," Gisèle admitted. "She wanted to inform the members of the association of her decision to spend a year in the United States, of her engagement with M. de Chareilles, and of . . . of . . . a few other projects."

"What projects?"

"She wanted to reorganize the association. . . . She had just discovered a key was missing, and there was a computer file that had been erased by mistake. Mme Bertrand-Verdon held me responsible for both losses, and she told me I was incompetent. . . . In the evening I managed to recover the file on the computer, and I thought I should bring her a printout straight away. She was having dinner when I got to the inn, and not wanting to disturb her, I slid the pages under the door to her room."

"Why have you been keeping all this from us?"

"I didn't think it was important."

"Let us decide, if you please, what is or is not important," the inspector instructed her coolly. "You were aware, I suppose, of Mme Bertrand-Verdon's . . . eating habits?"

"Well, yes, more or less," Gisèle acknowledged, a little disconcerted by the question, but relieved to see the conversation diverted away from the subject of Yvonne.

"So you know that she took a number of medications, especially sleeping pills?"

"I know she suffered from insomnia," Gisèle said.

"And you, Mlle Dambert, do you suffer from insomnia?"

"Sometimes," she admitted.

"And do you take sleeping pills?"

"Very seldom."

"Very seldom," Inspector Foucheroux repeated, stressing each syllable equally. "On prescription?"

"My brother-in-law is a doctor," she offered in response. She was suddenly reminded of a game of Ping-Pong.

"It's very convenient to have a doctor in the family, isn't it? In your opinion, what would he have to say about the heavy dose of Halcion that we found in the rose-petal jam that — as you know — Mme Bertrand-Verdon was in the habit of eating every evening? A dose that could have been fatal for anyone who was not . . . accustomed to the drug?"

"I don't know," Gisèle said softly. A strand of her scarf's black fringe snapped off in her fingers.

"Oh, but I believe you do know, Mlle Dambert. You're

181

the one who mixed the Halcion powder into the jam that Mme Bertrand-Verdon later consumed at about ten o'clock, as was her custom. We have a witness. All I want to hear from you is: why?"

Gisèle took another sip of water and took a deep breath. "I wanted her to sleep," she answered resolutely. "She'd had a bad day, and it was partly my fault. I felt responsible. . . . I wasn't sure she would take her medication, and whenever she didn't take it —"

"Whenever she didn't take it, her manic-depressive nature rose to the surface," he concluded for her. "And you were afraid she would make a scene. What I want to know is why."

"I wanted her to sleep," Gisèle said again. "There's no law against —"

"That's a nice cliché, Mlle Dambert, but a little inappropriate under the circumstances, wouldn't you say? It's true that Mme Bertrand-Verdon wasn't killed by an overdose of soporifics, but your action and that of the killer are most certainly connected in some way. How? We can't yet say for sure, but it's only a matter of time and patience before we can. We'll take this up again this evening. In the meantime I'll have to ask that you not make any attempt to leave the village. Otherwise I would be obliged to make use of the legal means at my disposal to assure your compliance. By the way, how did you get back to Paris yesterday evening?"

"By car," Gisèle let slip. "I hitched a ride," she added hurriedly in an attempt to cover her mistake.

"You hitched a ride, did you?" he said mockingly. "And can you give us the name and address of the driver who picked you up?" She shook her head slowly from side to side. "Can you describe the vehicle?" he insisted. She pressed her lips more tightly together. "It's just as I thought," said Foucheroux evenly. "Under these circumstances, I think it best that you accompany me now to Aunt Léonie's, where we are both expected. Will you come and join us there when you're done, Detective?"

"Certainly, Inspector," said Leila Djemani.

Gisèle got up and walked obediently out the door that Foucheroux held open for her.

Alone in the room, Leila put on a pair of latex gloves, carefully took hold of the glass of water she had given Gisèle, and put it in a plastic bag. The young woman had grown noticeably more confident toward the end of the interrogation, and Leila couldn't help wondering what she had been afraid they might ask in the course of this conversation that had been instructive less for what was said than for what had remained unspoken.

Before she went to join the group of visitors assembled in the entryway to Aunt Léonie's, Leila was seen in the company of an officer from the Criminal Investigation Department carrying out some odd-looking procedures on the shiny handle of the door of a brand-new Renault parked on Lemoine Square.

21

AT EXACTLY TWO-THIRTY in the afternoon, André Larivière, his blue bow tie firmly in place, his white hair
pasted to his head with an abundance of brilliantine,
strode to the front of a group of attentive and shivering ad-
mirers of Marcel Proust and began the guided tour of Aunt
Léonie's house by reciting his familiar quotation: *It is not
by visiting his birthplace or his place of death that one pays tribute
to a great man, but by traveling to the places he most
admired. . . .*

It soon became clear from his presentation that although neither the birth nor the death of Marcel Proust
had occurred in the house of his paternal aunt Élisabeth
Proust Amiot, the writer's choice of vocation was without
a doubt directly attributable to the brief visits he had
made here as a child during the holidays, before his first
outbreak of asthma. "Without Élisabeth Amiot," the guide
asserted forcefully, "there would have been no Aunt
Léonie. And without Ernestine, the elderly maid whose
photograph you will be able to observe in the kitchen, to

your left upon entering, there would have been no Françoise. . . ." And the astonishing inventory of parallels went on and on, between the village church and Saint-Hilaire in *Combray,* the priest in Proust's day and the curé in the novel, the river Loir and the river Vivonne, each comparison duly documented by a recitation of the corresponding passage in Proust's masterpiece. The guide grew more impassioned the more skeptical his listeners looked, especially when he asserted that, without the memory of this particular house, Proust would never have written his *Remembrance of Things Past.* Standing behind him, Gisèle smiled politely, and when they arrived in the kitchen — *little temple of Venus, overflowing with the offerings of the dairymaid, the fruiterer, the vegetable merchant* — she pointed at the various objects as the old man enumerated them.

Standing just behind the group, Foucheroux kept an eye on Patrick Rainsford and Guillaume Verdaillan, carefully observing their every move. Looking about to die of boredom, the American professor was clearly unmoved by the passages the old guide recited with such fervor. It was obvious that he had not come as a tourist, nor as a fan of Marcel Proust — unlike the others, who were standing, filled with wonder at the sanctum sanctorum, with their books open in front of them, as if at mass. While Verdaillan was busily playing the role of the easygoing, smiling Parisian intellectual, Foucheroux caught Rainsford casting furtive glances in the direction of the staircase, and when André Larivière launched forth into the passage about how *the hateful staircase I always climbed so dejectedly exhaled a smell of varnish that had come to incorporate or to represent the particular feeling of distress I experienced each evening,* the American professor, whose discomfort was becoming more than evident as he shifted nervously from one foot to the other, suddenly broke away from the group and walked off toward the little sitting room. It looked quite as though he had been unable to contain his scorn at the guide's interpretation of a passage that, as the old man explained, threw new light on the narrator's relationship to his father: *The wall on which I saw the glow of his candle as he ascended the staircase has long since been destroyed.* "Here, ladies and gentlemen, Marcel Proust is alluding to the house where he was born, in Auteuil. This house was destroyed . . ."

Out of the corner of his eye, Foucheroux saw Leila Djemani appear at the end of the hallway and motioned her over. "Mission accomplished," she whispered. "We've got the fingerprints."

"Perfect," he whispered back. "Rainsford is in the sitting room. Perhaps this would be a good time —"

"I'll take care of it. The only one left is Philippe Desforge, since we have M. de Chareilles's handkerchief."

"Neither of them is here," he said quietly.

Gisèle, whose pleasant voice had now replaced that of the old guide, was applying her remarkably clear diction to the passage detailing the furnishings in Aunt Léonie's room — *On the side of her bed stood a yellow lemon-wood chest and a table that served both as a dispensary and a high altar* — since the "tragic occurrences," as André Larivière had pointed out on several occasions, prevented them from going to see them for themselves. Foucheroux was transfixed by the metamorphosis of the shy young woman into a passionate lover of words whose voice and intonation clearly showed a profound understanding of the text, and he scarcely noticed when Leila Djemani left him and walked to the little sitting room into which Patrick Rainsford had disappeared a moment earlier.

"Oh!" she cried in feigned surprise at finding Professor Rainsford standing in contemplation in front of the photograph of the three Amiot brothers.

By way of greeting, Rainsford made a derogatory remark about the poor taste of the middle class in fin-de-siècle France by poking fun at the little lectern for the Koran in front of the fireplace and at the outlandish predilection for things oriental that had obviously dictated the choice of the two paintings on the walls. "No offense intended, of course," he added, suddenly realizing that his remark had transgressed the most elementary tenets of political correctness.

"Of course," Leila forced herself to say. "They say this room has been left exactly as it was when Proust came here as a child. The wallpaper, the candelabra, the window in the door — here, I've got an old photograph." He grabbed the postcard she held out to him and gave it a distracted glance.

"Indeed," he said as he handed it back to her, oblivious to the fingerprints he had just delivered into her hands.

"And the door is really very nice, with its red and blue window," Leila persisted. "When it's sunny out, it must give a charming view of the little garden."

"Is that so?" he said curtly, glancing mechanically out the little window. All of a sudden his head jerked forward convulsively, and, his hands shaking, he reached for the back of an armchair to keep from falling. "The sta— sta— sta—," he stammered uncontrollably, gaping openly at the round patch of black dirt in the middle of which he had clearly expected to see the little gracious and smiling figure of the statue.

"Is this your first visit?" Leila asked as though nothing had happened, carefully putting the postcard away between two sheets of tracing paper in her bag.

But Rainsford had completely recovered his presence of mind. Somewhat pale but perfectly self-confident, he turned and looked her straight in the eye. "It's certainly my last, I'll tell you that," he said rather arrogantly, cleverly avoiding her question. "In my country, we have progressed far beyond the biographical method of criticism, and we don't set a lot of store in literary pilgrimages. Now, if you would excuse me, I would like to go rejoin the others."

"But of course," Leila said evenly.

He went off toward the dining room, where the assembly was listening to André Larivière continue his presentation. "In *Jean Santeuil,* that early sketch of the masterpiece that we all know, we have an exact description of this dining room," the guide was explaining. "And to show you just what I mean, let me read you this passage: *But on the days when Jean wanted to spend a long time reading before lunch . . .*"

Leila squeezed in next to Foucheroux. "Got 'em," she said in his ear. "He didn't notice a thing. The only one left is Philippe Desforge."

"Good," he whispered. "He isn't here. There's no point in waiting any longer. Send everything off to the lab, top priority."

As Leila left the room to carry out this last order, the guide was just concluding his speech, his voice vibrant with emotion. "But it is in *Swann's Way* that we find a description of the lamp you see before you." Everyone looked up at the candelabra suspended above the table as the guide intoned for their benefit: *The reassuring glow of the hanging lamp that . . . was so well acquainted with his parents and the customary pot of beef stew!* Exhausted, he wiped the sweat from his forehead and waved his hand theatrically to cede the floor to Gisèle, who in a compelling voice invited the group to take a quick stroll through the garden. It was, she claimed, but one of several different places the author had used in constructing the "garden of Combray" — a comment that earned her a livid glance from André Larivière, who was firmly convinced that the original garden was here and nowhere else.

Inspector Foucheroux went out first to choose his observation post. He stood on the little stoop leading up to the back door of the kitchen, next to the water pump, his feet planted firmly on one of the salamander heads in the pattern on the chipped tiles. The little group spread out in a circle, some admiring the trellis, some "recognizing" the iron table, the bench, the wicker chair where the narrator of the novel sits down to read. Others were paying homage to the enormous linden tree or the old lantern suspended above the glass door to the orangery. A smiling Professor Rainsford was enlightening a pretty young blond as to the etymology of the verb "to bloom."

"Give them the passages on the mornings spent reading in the garden," André Larivière commanded. "Pages 297 and 309," he snapped impatiently as Gisèle opened her book. Suddenly his faded gaze fell on the empty space in the middle of the flower bed. "The scoundrels!" he shouted. "They've stolen books, they've stolen pictures, they've stolen curtains — but a statue! That beats everything!"

Detective Djemani started to rush over to calm the old man, whose face was flushed with anger, when she saw Foucheroux raise a forefinger discreetly to his lips and stopped in time to let Gisèle Dambert allay the guide's fears. "No one stole the statue, M. Larivière. Théodore put it inside yesterday, because of the frost. I asked him to bring it to the office."

"No one ever tells me anything," André Larivière grumbled to the person standing closest to him, who happened to be Guillaume Verdaillan. "Now we won't be able to read —"

"The passages about the statues. What a pity," the professor said sympathetically.

"I see that you're a connoisseur yourself, monsieur," the guide said appreciatively as Gisèle, following his orders, went about breathing new life into the words of the text: *On these temperate days, when Jean awoke, he went down to the garden.* . . . Then, as though to tease the old guide, she strayed from her instructions and read the passage on the chestnut tree: *Seated in the back of a little grass and canvas hut, hidden, I believed, from the gaze of anyone who might come to visit my parents.* . . .

"I'll wager she's going to forget to ring the bell for them," André Larivière murmured under his breath. He cut his way through the crowd and took up his position next to the green gate that opened onto Lemoine Square, determined to engrave into the memory of the visitors the *discordant, ferruginous, and icy sound* that signals Swann's arrival in the first volume of *Remembrance of Things Past.* He was right in the midst of his reflection when Philippe Desforge's shadowy outline appeared in the doorway opposite him. As colorless as ever, his face as pale as ashes, his hands and wrists cloaked in leather gloves, the associate publisher of Martin-Dubois Press walked over and exchanged a few words with Gisèle, who nodded her head in agreement. After ringing the little iron bell three times, duly recorded by a number of portable cassette players, André Larivière suggested reluctantly that they conclude the visit in the little sitting room before giving the visitors an opportunity to purchase some of the myriad Proustian mementos that were available in the reception room.

As he walked by Inspector Foucheroux, Patrick Rainsford remarked loudly to his blond acquaintance that the French police, who had lost all respect for a person's bereavement, had prevented him from rushing to the bed-side of his expiring grandmother.

"What a liar," another blond girl giggled to a third. "I heard him on the phone this morning asking someone to send him a telegram pretending that his grandmother had died!"

Foucheroux stepped up to Rainsford's right as Leila fell into step to his left, placing herself adroitly between him and the girl. "Would you come with us, please?" the inspector said quietly.

Professor Rainsford didn't open his mouth all the way to the police station. Only when he was seated in the little room where Gisèle Dambert had been interrogated earlier that afternoon did he say, "I won't speak except in the presence of my lawyer."

The consulate had recommended he cooperate with the French police but had advised him as well that he did have the right, as a foreign national, to be represented by an accredited attorney if he were involved in a difficult legal situation. The secretary had then given him a list of names that was considerably shortened by the fact that he had insisted his lawyer be bilingual — quite a rarity in the countryside of France. In fact, the only acceptable name on the list was Cyrille Laucournet, when it was explained that he had worked for a year in Washington at the law offices of Weisberg, Herman and Mikalson.

"I demand to speak with M. Cyrille Laucournet," the professor announced stridently. Foucheroux and Leila exchanged a knowing look of annoyance, then acquiesced to his demand.

Cyrille Laucournet, Esq., arrived an hour later, radiating importance, competence, and dignity with his three-piece suit, horn-rimmed glasses, and leather briefcase. He asked immediately to confer with his client in private. The consultation lasted just long enough for the laboratory to call in with the preliminary results of the tests that had been carried out on the objects sent in that afternoon. Foucheroux was gratified to learn that the statue did indeed appear to be the murder weapon. It had been scrubbed with soap and water, but the cleaning turned out to have been less than thorough and had left several traces of type-O blood and a few hairs, indubitably belonging to the victim. Two partial fingerprints had been identified as belonging to Patrick Rainsford and Gisèle Dambert. The results of the final analysis would be sent on as soon as possible.

Armed with this information, Inspector Foucheroux and Detective Djemani walked with newfound confidence into the little room where Patrick Rainsford and his lawyer were still conversing.

"I must inform you," the inspector said sternly, "that there have been some new developments. Not only do we have a witness, a Mlle Ferrand, student in comparative literature, who is willing to testify that she overheard you, M. Rainsford, ask your brother to send you a telegram calling you back to the United States when you spoke to him on the phone this morning at the Aigneaux farm, but the laboratory has just notified us that your fingerprints were found on the murder weapon. Would you care to explain?"

Cyrille Laucournet leaned over toward his client and must have whispered some encouraging words, for Rainsford suddenly sat up straight and declared in a firm voice, "I am not guilty."

"Of what?" Foucheroux asked softly.

"Of murdering Adeline Bertrand-Verdon. I'm not the one who killed her."

"Then why are you trying to flee?" the inspector asked pointedly.

"Precisely to avoid finding myself in a situation like this!" the professor said, a note of irritation in his voice. "Abroad, with an archaic legal system —" A little cough from his lawyer warned him to leave off this dangerous tack. "I wanted to avoid making things more complicated than they really are," he said lamely.

"By distorting the facts?"

Patrick Rainsford threw a questioning glance at his lawyer and, unable to get a word out, squirmed on his seat like an adolescent accused of having neglected his chores.

"By putting us on the wrong track?" Inspector Foucheroux went on implacably.

Rainsford opened his mouth and closed it again without making the slightest sound, looking strangely like some precious exotic fish dumped out of the temperate water of its deluxe aquarium.

"Suppose you just tell us what really happened, now, so as to . . . avoid — since that seems to be your favorite word — being charged with obstructing justice," the inspector suggested smoothly.

Seeing his lawyer nod, Rainsford cleared his throat. "As to the last time I saw Mme Bertrand-Verdon . . . ," he began hesitantly. "Um . . . I had an appointment to see her that night, after dinner, to finalize the announcement of her plans to come to the United States. . . ." Feeling not unlike a high diver perched on the edge of a bottomless void, he paused, swallowed, and took the plunge: "At the last minute, she told me she had some urgent business that required her presence at Aunt Léonie's house. When she didn't come back, I decided to go and meet her. . . ."

"What time was that?" asked Inspector Foucheroux,

taking advantage of a slight pause to put in his question as unobtrusively as possible.

"At about eleven-thirty, I guess." Rainsford pushed back an unruly lock that persisted in falling forward onto his forehead. "I went straight to Aunt Léonie's. When I got there, everything was dark, but the door wasn't locked. I went in. I called out to Mme Bertrand-Verdon several times. I heard no response, and I went up to the first floor. When I got there —" He was overcome with an uncontrollable shudder at the memory of what happened next. Foucheroux and Leila Djemani sat perfectly still. It was Cyrille Laucournet who, with a single blink of his eyelids, encouraged his client to continue his account. "The door to the office was wide open. It was pitch-black. I went in and I . . . I lost my balance, I slipped on something . . . something wet. When I tried to cushion my fall, my hand touched . . . the statue. It was lying on the floor next to Adeline Bertrand-Verdon. I put my hand in the blood that was all over the bottom of the statue." His arms jerked back uncontrollably. "I panicked," he conceded with a gulp. "I thought people would think . . . with my fingerprints on the statue, I was afraid I'd be . . ." He broke off. "I took it to the bathroom across the hall and washed it in lots of water, and then I . . . then I put it back in its place, in the garden," he concluded in a sheepish voice.

"You do realize that your actions could be construed as a deliberate attempt to obstruct the progress of a criminal investigation by tampering with the evidence?"

At this point Cyrille Laucournet, adjusting his glasses, spoke up to plead his client's cause in lofty terms, as though he were already in court. Spouting legal jargon and alleging his client's state of mental exhaustion, he obtained his immediate release.

"Do you really think he's telling the truth?" Leila asked skeptically as soon as they were gone.

"Certainly not the whole truth," he said. "But I'm tempted to believe the story about the statue. And I don't think there's any great danger in leaving him in the custody of M. Laucournet for the time being. Let's move on to Guillaume Verdaillan, who must be fuming with impatience. That is, if you're absolutely sure that Philippe Desforge and Gisèle Dambert are waiting for us at the inn."

"That's what I instructed them to do, following your orders," Leila said, somewhat surprised by the inspector's anxious concern. "Do you want me to go and make sure?"

"That's not a bad idea. Why don't you do just that, if you don't mind. . . ."

*

Alone, Foucheroux tried to analyze objectively the reasons for his anxiety. Something kept running around in his head, something almost unconscious — a thought he was incapable of expressing, an image he couldn't quite put together in his mind. He rubbed his knee. He was not at all reassured when Detective Djemani came back and told him, a smile on her face, that the two other "witnesses" were quietly ensconced in their rooms, one of them reading a book, the other taking a nap, and that as expected, Professor Verdaillan was smoking, ranting, and raving in the waiting room, much to the distress of Sergeant Tournadre.

It was ten past six.

Night had fallen.

22

THE ATMOSPHERE in Aunt Léonie's house became noticeably more relaxed as soon as Inspector Foucheroux and Detective Djemani had left. All that remained to remind the little group of the tragic events was a boyish-looking officer posted on the landing to keep overly curious visitors from walking up the stairs. For the most part the conventioneers were satisfied with their visit to the land of Proust in its abbreviated version and felt no inclination to venture onto the second floor. One elderly lady who seemed to be from England complained of a corn on her foot, and another woman did grumble briefly about coming all the way from Holland only to be prevented from seeing Marcel's childhood bedroom, but after all, the convention had taken place, and they had all been given a partial tour of the house, in spite of the circumstances.

After finishing his official presentation with an unabashed plug for the souvenirs displayed on the table in front of them, André Larivière treated everyone to a dozen different anecdotes about the history of the village, complained at length about the delinquency of the Landmarks Commission in keeping the house in good repair, enumerated the various names of the village streets over a half dozen centuries, and recalled how, in the Middle Ages, the pilgrims had passed through on their way to Saint-Jacques-de-Compostelle. A number of visitors took his picture. After the last of them had left, he merrily counted up the day's receipts, penny by penny.

His worst fears — the untimely arrival of Ray Taylor's camera team or an invasion of local and Parisian reporters — had proved groundless, but there was no foretelling the future, and he was afraid that the noble appeal of Aunt Léonie's as a literary historical monument might be temporarily eclipsed by its unhealthy allure as the scene of the president's murder. On the other hand, an increase in the number of visitors would do a lot to improve the finances of the association, which had been put in a dangerous state by the reckless administration of Mme Bertrand-Verdon. The woman had suffered from delusions of grandeur.

Just as he was about to ask Gisèle Dambert, Guillaume Verdaillan, and Philippe Desforge, who were jabbering away in the corner, to allow him to bring the day's visit to a close, he saw the tall, dark immigrant who called herself a police detective reappear in the room as though out of thin air. He heard her summon Guillaume Verdaillan to the police station and instruct the other two to return to the Old Mill Inn and remain there until they received further word from the police. He gave a sigh of relief when Gisèle Dambert accepted Philippe Desforge's offer to drive her back to the inn. Aunt Léonie's house was about to recover the peace, the dignity, and the sanctity it should never have been deprived of in the first place. He had

197

never really trusted those two anyway, and all things considered, he was not inclined to linger in the company of one — or even two — violent criminals!

*

Guillaume Verdaillan sped off in a foul humor, leaving Gisèle to drive back to the hotel with Philippe Desforge in his Peugeot, a less luxurious but, Gisèle felt, infinitely more secure means of transportation than the professor's Renault. They drove the few miles to the inn without exchanging a word. Philippe Desforge, his hands sheathed in a pair of driving gloves that struck an odd contrast to the rest of his attire, was clearly concentrating on the road. Adeline had often spoken of him condescendingly, even disparagingly, and Gisèle had always found him pathetically courteous and overly solicitous. She preferred to forget what she had overheard a couple of times when she had come upon the two of them unexpectedly. As a good Proustian, she could understand why he had subjected himself to such humiliation: in romance, who loves loses, and this man on the verge of old age had loved Adeline to the point of sacrificing for her his own self-respect. "There's a Swann in all of us," she thought.

It was, therefore, out of sympathy for this man who had lost everything that she accepted his invitation to stay a moment and chat with him before going back upstairs. The Old Mill Inn prided itself on its tearoom, which tempted its patrons with an assortment of homemade pastries — succulent *palmier* biscuits, mocha eclairs, napoleons, fruit pies — to go along with its select Chinese, Russian, and Indian teas.

"Adeline really knew how to brew tea," Philippe Desforge

said with a sigh, waving "no" with his leather-gloved hand to a young waitress who came up with a tray of petits fours.

"That was indeed one of her talents," Gisèle was able to agree without bending the truth.

"What are you going to do now, Mlle Dambert?" he asked with a concern that took her somewhat by surprise. He had never shown any interest in her situation before.

"I'm not quite sure, but I'd like to defend my thesis as quickly as possible."

"Under Verdaillan? He has a reputation for . . . how should I put it . . . profiting from his student's research."

"He's not going to profit from mine," Gisèle said with more bitterness in her voice than she had intended to show. She raised her cup of Darjeeling to her lips.

"Mlle Dambert," he said softly, "I must tell you that I" — he leaned forward and put his cup back down on its saucer, revealing the ugly red splotches on his wrists — "know all about the notebooks."

Gisèle was so surprised she jerked involuntarily, spilling her tea onto her skirt. "Excuse me," she mumbled, and walked off toward the restrooms, less to clean up the spill than to reevaluate the situation in private. When she reemerged from the ladies' room a few minutes later, the spot on her skirt had almost disappeared, and she had made up her mind to tell him the whole filthy truth, both about the way she had been swindled and about the pact she had concluded with her doctoral advisor.

*

By the time he was finally escorted to the room where the other witnesses had been questioned before him, Professor Verdaillan was livid with anger. He swore to himself that anyone who kept an eminent professor of the University of Paris at Neuilly waiting for such a length of time would not go unpunished, and he had already composed in his mind a good part of the letter of complaint he intended to write to the police commissioner. This little inspector and his ridiculous assistant would both be hauled over the coals. Nevertheless, in his heart of hearts he knew that his fit of anger at the outside world was really aimed at hiding another emotion he was less inclined to acknowledge: fear. Guillaume Verdaillan was afraid of finding out that despite their agreement and his own threats, Gisèle Dambert had talked.

"Please have a seat, Professor," Inspector Foucheroux said amiably.

"It's a little late for such displays of courtesy," Verdaillan replied angrily. "Do you realize how long you've kept me waiting?"

"Long enough for us to question the other witnesses. Please accept my apologies. . . ." He paused for a moment. "Allow me to come back to a certain point of detail. You have stated that you were the first to leave Mme Bertrand-Verdon after dinner on the evening in question. Do you still affirm this to be the case?"

"First, second, what's the difference?" Guillaume Verdaillan retorted impertinently.

"What's the difference?" the inspector said evenly. "Let's say . . . the difference between the possibility of being charged with murder — and the simple questioning of a witness who is ready to cooperate with the police. Your choice."

The remark hit home. Guillaume Verdaillan felt about mechanically for his cigarettes but decided to give up the search when he caught sight of Detective Djemani's warning glare. "I was the third to leave Mme Bertrand-Verdon. M. de Chareilles left first, followed by Patrick Rainsford."

"Are you sure?"

"Completely."

"And you didn't see Mlle Dambert?"

Uh-oh, the professor said to himself, here's the trap. He decided to play dumb. "Mlle Dambert? Of course not. She wasn't at the dinner. Why on earth would I have seen her? You heard her yourself the next day when she asked for an appointment to talk with me —"

"She told us —," the inspector began cautiously.

"—about her dissertation," Leila Djemani put in, acting on an impulse.

The effect these few words produced on the famous professor was spectacular. His shoulders drooped, his hands started to tremble uncontrollably, and a look of defeat replaced the arrogant facade he had kept up until then. "So you know," he stammered, the victim of his own fears.

"We do indeed," Foucheroux said sternly, without the slightest idea what the professor was talking about. He avoided exchanging glances with Leila. "But we want to give you a chance to tell your side of the story."

"I don't know where to start," Guillaume Verdaillan said with a sigh. "I guess everything began the day Mme Bertrand-Verdon told me she had found the 1905 notebooks. . . ." He paused. Inspector Foucheroux and Detective Djemani nodded simultaneously, as though they knew perfectly well what he was referring to. "You can imagine what a threat this . . . discovery posed to my edition of Marcel Proust's complete works, at a time when . . . well, at a critical juncture for Proust studies as a whole." Foucheroux and Leila nodded again, knowing full well that it was a critical time less for Proust studies as a whole than for the reputation of the editor of his complete works. "Mme Bertrand-Verdon suggested we come to some sort of . . . compromise." He had a hard time getting out the last word. "She offered to serve as my coeditor. But I was opposed to this idea even before I knew to whom the notebooks really belonged. I've always believed that in order to preserve a semblance of unity, a critical edition should be prepared by a single scholar working on his own," he said, unable to resist a digression that would allow him to trot out his old battle horse — even with his own freedom at stake. "So I cast about for some means of making Mme Bertrand-Verdon understand all the unfortunate consequences a joint effort would entail. But she simply would not listen to reason, and she insisted on announcing the new arrangement at the convention. . . ." Inspector Foucheroux and Detective Djemani exchanged a knowing glance, the meaning of which did not for a moment escape Professor Verdaillan. "You can be sure that this point of contention between us gave me an excellent motive for wishing her gone, but I soon found the perfect means of making Mme Bertrand-Verdon give up her editorial ambitions for good," he continued, surprised by the ease with which he could now speak. "Purely by chance, I attended a dinner last week to which Max Brachet-Léger, the critic, had been invited as well. We all had a little too much to drink, and he himself was in a particularly jolly state, if I may say so. Over dessert he told us, among other things, that he had gone to school with Adeline Verdon and had known her first husband extremely well. It was quite a shock to learn that she had been married at all, and to a . . . uh . . . friend of M. Brachet-Léger. You can imagine the effect such a disclosure would have had on someone like M. de Chareilles, for example."

"I can indeed," said Inspector Foucheroux, who understood only too well this particular method of giving the doctor a taste of his own medicine. "And you told Mme Bertrand-Verdon about your . . . discovery?"

"I intended to do so," Professor Verdaillan acknowledged without a trace of shame, "but she wasn't in her room after dinner, and I decided to put it off till the next morning. I had no way of knowing that by that time she would . . . no longer be with us."

"Nor that her death would do nothing to solve the problem, since the notebooks were not hers after all," Leila Djemani put in on an almost imperceptible signal from her superior.

"I would have discovered sooner or later that they belonged to Mlle Dambert," Verdaillan said with a degree of self-satisfaction. "But she's my student, after all. Students are easy enough to manage. At any rate, now that the alleged notebooks have disappeared a second time, she hasn't got a shred of tangible proof. Her thesis is reduced to a tall tale of lost manuscripts discovered in a drawer, spirited away by an unscrupulous boss, recovered in a midnight break-in, only to be stolen in the end by a group of Italian tourists. You must agree that her story isn't worth a red penny."

"Doubtless, especially compared with the financial and critical value of the edition of the century," Inspector Foucheroux replied dryly.

"That's what Philippe Desforge thought," said Guillaume Verdaillan, oblivious to the irony of the inspector's last remark. "He wants to bury this whole business about the notebooks and get on with the edition of the complete works as soon as possible. It's in his interest, after all, as much as mine."

"How's that?"

"Oh, well, it's no secret that his job at Martin-Dubois is hanging by a thread, now that he's left Mathilde. He's staked everything on this Proust edition, and lately he's been in such a nervous state that his eczema has been plaguing him more than ever. It's gotten to the point that —"

"That will be all, Professor Verdaillan, thank you very much," said Foucheroux suddenly, standing up so abruptly that he knocked his chair over backward. "Sergeant Tournadre will ask you to sign your statement."

As soon as they were in the hallway, he glanced back at Leila Djemani, who was gaping at him in astonishment, and said, "Gisèle Dambert is in danger."

*

After her conversation with Philippe Desforge, Gisèle went back to her room feeling so exhausted that, against her habits, she lay down on her bed fully dressed. She had to gird herself for a final confrontation with the police. She noticed a bouquet of fresh flowers in a blue vase, reminding her of the flowers that often figured in Yvonne's paintings. She gave up trying to keep her sister's name from emerging out of the depths of her unconscious. Before facing the police, she was going to have to face what she had found out from Yvonne.

Sitting in the office that night, Yvonne had confided everything in her, pouring out revelation after revelation about her marvelous lover, and about life behind the scenes with Jacques. "You have no idea how boring it is to be a doctor's wife, Gisèle. . . . All those endless dinner parties with a bunch of old farts who spout off a lot of incomprehensible words in order to talk about the most ordinary things! And all this traveling —"

"I thought you loved to travel," Gisèle put in encouragingly.

"Yeah, sure, I like to travel. But when you've seen the Pyramids twice, New York five or six times, and Tokyo once too many, you get tired of it. And foreign languages really aren't my thing, I don't have to tell you that. I'd almost rather stay all by myself in my studio."

"And the children?"

"The children, the children . . . they'll grow up. They really don't need me very much, what with school, ski courses, vacations with their grandparents and their cousins. And there's always Jane to take care of any problems that come up. My life was so empty before . . ." She gazed dreamily toward the ceiling. "The simple truth is that I married too young. I didn't have time to get a real taste of life. Jacques is very nice, I'm not blaming him for anything, but he's not . . . you know . . . very romantic, and he's not . . . um . . . well, we never really got along all that terribly well, physically, I mean. . . ."

Gisèle was dumbstruck. She remembered as though it were yesterday the way Yvonne and Jacques had held hands during their engagement, how they couldn't help gazing at each other amorously, even in public, how they had rejoiced at the birth of their children. If there had ever been a couple that seemed happy together, it was Yvonne and Jacques! Recovering her voice, she forced herself to ask: "And the man you met . . . He's romantic?"

"Totally, totally . . ."

And Yvonne launched off on a detailed description of all the romantic exploits she'd experienced with the rare bird who had shown her what it really meant to be a woman. "Everything from Emma Bovary to *Cosmopolitan*," Gisèle couldn't help thinking as she interrupted her sister's near-pornographic account to suggest it was time they

205

started getting back to Paris, after stopping off at the Old Mill Inn. Submerged in her own interior world, Yvonne wasn't even curious when her sister told her to park behind the large trees that shielded the hotel from the road. She sat patiently in the driver's seat, and when Gisèle reappeared ten minutes later and told her to start the car and drive off as quietly as possible, she took up her sentence exactly where she had left it.

"We met exactly three months, seven days, and" — she glanced at the gold face of the Tiffany watch her husband had given her for her last birthday — "two hours ago. At a physician's conference in Vienna, of all places. When I think I almost didn't go! But luckily there was a Klimt retrospective. That's what made up my mind for me. And it was there, in front of *The Kiss*, that he kissed me for the first time —"

"Keep your eyes on the road," Gisèle murmured involuntarily. Fully absorbed in her memories, her sister had swerved dangerously close to the narrow highway's crumbling shoulder.

"We've been seeing each other as much as we can, but I simply cannot go on living without him," Yvonne asserted, jerking the wheel to the left in a show of determination.

"Are you really going to leave Jacques and the children?"

"That's where I need your help, Gisèle. For the time being, I'm going to rent a little apartment by myself, you know, a one- or two-bedroom place on the Left Bank, where he'll come and join me whenever he can."

"So he's not . . . single?" She had to struggle to get the last word across her lips.

"In the process of getting a divorce," Yvonne said cheerily, as though it were the most natural thing in the world. "His wife is a horrible shrew who thinks about nothing but money. . . ."

Of course she's a shrew, Gisèle said to herself. She stopped listening to the litany of clichés her sister was spouting off with so much pleasure and drifted off until the words "tonight, tonight" brought her back to the present.

"Tonight was the night I'd planned to tell Jacques, but he had an emergency at the hospital. It's just like him," Yvonne said bitterly.

"It might be a little imprudent to burn all your bridges before you really have to. Why not tell him you need a little time to think? Why not try a temporary separation for the sake of the children's future? Wait a little. . . ."

"I should have known you wouldn't understand, Little Miss Scaredy-Cat," Yvonne said indignantly. "Poor Gisèle, always so timid. I tell you I've met the man of my dreams, and you tell me to wait. Wait for what?"

"For things to get a little less confusing."

"Nothing is confusing. The situation is as clear as day," Yvonne shot back, tossing her blond hair with an impatient shake of her head. "I love him, he loves me, we want to live together. . . . Of course, we have to be careful not to scare off his patients. He's quite well known in psychiatric circles. He's published a lot of very controversial things, and he can't go around making himself vulnerable to an attack on his personal life."

Suddenly Gisèle had a horrible suspicion. "What's his name?"

"Selim. Selim Malik." Yvonne seemed to be in awe of his very name. Then, mistaking her sister's horrified silence for an expression of disapproval, she added hotly, "He's Lebanese and from a Christian family, if that's what you want to know. He's a psychiatrist at Sainte-Anne. He's a vegetarian, and he loves Corelli. Just like you."

"Stop the car immediately," Gisèle managed to say. She was about to be sick to her stomach.

"Oh, that's great, Gisèle, perfect time to get sick, just when, for once in my life, I ask you to help!" Yvonne burst out without the least sympathy in her voice.

What had happened next was all muddled up in Gisèle's memory. The drive from Chartres to Paris had seemed endless, and she had felt utterly incapable of giving her sister the moral and material support she said she needed. Gisèle couldn't remember what strategy she had used to extract from Yvonne the promise to go home and not to say anything until the end of the week.

After Yvonne had let her out on the rue des Plantes, Gisèle had taken a cab to the rue Saint-Anselme, crept like a thief into Adeline's apartment, opened her safe with the little key she had stolen from her earlier, and recovered, amid repeated heaves of her stomach, the fifteen notebooks that were her property.

Stretched out on the comfortable bed in room twenty-five of the Old Mill Inn and exhausted by the memory of this ghastly night, Gisèle drifted off to sleep. She dreamt that she was standing at the foot of a long staircase, listening to the muffled sounds of laughter and Italian baroque music coming from a closed door at the top of the stairs. The sounds lured her to the second floor. When she reached the door, she found herself submerged in the artificial darkness and hushed silence of a theater, filled with the sounds of gowns rustling, of paper being crumpled, of people whispering in scarcely audible tones, of an orchestra tuning up to play. Suddenly the door in front of her changed into a red velvet curtain, and a dwarf with a ribald look in his eye pulled it back just far enough to open a thin crack. On a large round bed in the middle of a room, the walls of which were made of mirror, she saw Yvonne's flowing blond hair spread out on Selim's bare chest. . . . She saw their fingers clasp, their lips touch.

"No!" she screamed. "No!" But it was too late. She wanted to go back, but a wall of glass blocked her way. She was caught. She put her hand over her eyes, but she couldn't help hearing the heavy breathing becoming faster and faster, culminating in a guttural groan she had heard before.

The rustling of a sheet of paper being pushed under her door woke her with a start. Her cheeks burning, she jumped out of bed, snatched up the little rectangle of paper that lay glimmering in the half-light, and read: "Found bag. Meet me at the Mirougrain pond at seven. Albert."

It was twenty past six.

She didn't have a minute to lose.

23

"MLLE DAMBERT IS GONE."

The words Inspector Foucheroux most dreaded hearing were uttered with complete tranquillity by the proprietress of the Old Mill Inn, who was busy going over the reservations for that evening's dinner. "She went on a walk, and she asked me to tell you she would be back around eight. She looked as if she was in a hurry."

"When did she leave?"

"At about six-thirty," the woman replied calmly. "Just after M. Desforge went out. He had a call from Paris. He left a message for you."

"Give it to me." Foucheroux made no effort to conceal his impatience.

"For heaven's sake, it's sitting right here in front of you," the proprietress said rather impertinently as she pulled an envelope with the hotel's letterhead out of a stack of papers.

He read it frantically, at the same time as Leila, who was looking over his shoulder.

Dear Inspector Foucheroux,

I have been called back to Paris on some urgent business. You can reach me this evening at Martin-Dubois Press (45 99 62 33.) Sorry I couldn't wait for you here.

Philippe Desforge

Foucheroux ran a weary hand across the tight little furrows spread across his brow and barked, "Give us the key to Mlle Dambert's room."

"But, Inspector, she took it with her," the proprietress said. "Since she said she would be coming back in just a few moments . . ."

"You have a copy? A master key?" the inspector asked. There was no mistaking the urgency in his voice.

"Well, yes, my husband has —"

"Go get it, quick. . . . It's a matter of life and death."

A few seconds later, Foucheroux and Leila Djemani opened the door to the room where Gisèle had been staying. They immediately saw the depression that her body had made in the mattress, as well as a rectangular sheet of paper lying open on the antique secretary. "Thank heavens!" murmured Foucheroux, as Leila, after reading the brief message, let slip a soft moan of distress.

"It's the same handwriting . . . ," she whispered.

She would never forget what happened next. Foucheroux, who hadn't so much as sat in a driver's seat for over three years, dashed off like a madman toward the car parked in front of the inn, grabbed the keys out of her hand, jumped in behind the wheel, and, suddenly recovering the skills he thought he had forgotten for good, raced off at breakneck speed toward the Mirougrain pond.

An hour earlier Gisèle had hurried along a series of crooked backwoods paths, trying to get to her curiously arranged meeting on time. She wondered how Albert had managed to recover her bag, and why he had chosen such an out-of-the-way place to give it back to her.

Mirougrain had a bad reputation. Toward the end of the last century a young woman of bizarre ways, Juliette Joinville d'Artois, had lived there as a recluse in the company of a deaf-mute male servant, an arrangement that had led to more than a little gossip. She had used the remains of the prehistoric dolmens strewn about the surrounding fields to decorate the exterior of her little house, which she referred to presumptuously as her "temple." The "Rock of Mirougrain," as the little island in the middle of the pond was called, still figured in rumors of devil worship, black masses, and bloody sacrifices, even though the house now belonged to a very respectable Parisian family that had made it their summer home. The pond was in fact a pocket of the Loir, and the island in it was connected to the mainland by a charming wooden bridge.

It was dark and cold. Gisèle followed a series of twisted and muddy paths that cut zigzags through the "fluvial region" that the narrator of *Remembrance of Things Past* generally situated, thanks to the meanderings of his fanciful topography, near the Guermantes estate. The drifting mists reminded her, by means of an unconscious quirk of her olfactory memory, of the rainy night spent roaming about the banks of the Seine on the black day she had seen Selim for the last time.

They had made a date for late afternoon at the Sarah Bernhardt Café. She had rehearsed the lines she would use to break the news to him countless times, she had bought a new dress in his favorite colors, and she was wearing the contact lenses that made her blue eyes appear dark brown, the way he liked them. When she told him she was expecting a baby, the pain his response had given her was sharper than anything a woman had ever felt during labor.

"From whom?" There was no irony in his voice.

A few seconds went by before she was able to make the slightest sound. The café reeled before her eyes, the pink and green drinks on the tables around her fusing together in an inextricable blur. She asked him if he was joking.

"No, I'm not joking. I have no idea what you do with your days — nor with most of your nights, for that matter. I don't spend my time checking up on you."

She told him it was his child.

He went through a number of elegant verbal pirouettes, the gist of which was that it was her problem, but he was willing, of course, to assume the financial responsibility of an abortion.

She started to cry.

Without a moment's hesitation he summoned the waiter with a peremptory wave of the hand, paid for their drinks, and stood up from the table. "You didn't honestly think I would —," he began. Then he shook his head three times, shrugged his shoulders as though to say there was nothing he could do, and walked straight out the door.

All she could see at that moment was a mass of circles and rings in a variety of colors. Inside the green ring of the table was the white ring of the saucer on which the waiter had left the little torn receipt. Another saucer formed a second white ring centered around the black circle of the coffee in the cup, and she sat for a long time staring into the pale yellow circle of her own glass, at the edge of which the imprint of her lips appeared in the form of a bright red arch.

She had walked around in circles all night long, back and forth over the damp bridges of the Seine, which smelled unpleasantly of mud and sludge. She was spared the horror of a decision when, three weeks later, she had accidentally tripped and fallen, losing the child and, nearly, her own life. She had never said anything to anyone, and now she was going to have to tell everything to Yvonne.

It was five past seven when Gisèle caught sight of the Mirougrain house on the small hill in the middle of the pond. She hadn't seen a soul along the path. It took her just a few minutes more to make her way to the little wooden platform that bridged the arm of the Loir. She walked across and peered into the darkness, looking for Albert's silhouette. The nauseating odor of the stagnant water, awash in dead roots, bits of rotting aquatic plants, and the remains of myriad tiny animals, rose up to meet her. She ventured onto the little wood plank that served as a kind of dock to get a better view of the island as a whole. Suddenly she heard a rustling of branches behind her, and she spun around to face the path that led to a little potting shed up above.

"Albert?" she called out in an uncertain voice. A moment later, her eyes opened wide with surprise as she recognized the person walking silently toward her. "You?"

She didn't understand what was happening to her until she fell backward into the still water, shoved off the dock by a pair of gloved hands whose strength she would never have imagined. Her heavy boots and her winter clothes pulled her straight down toward the muddy bottom. Her

214

hairpins came loose from the bun on her head and fanned out above her, sparkling like falling stars. The muddy taste of the icy water came rushing into her nose and mouth, and her hair, now undone, clung to her face like a deadly mass of algae. The monstrous underwater world with its tadpoles, its minnows, it water beetles, closed in around her like a fluid coffin. When I touch bottom, I'll push off with my feet and bounce back to the surface, she said to herself as rationally as she could. But it was her right shoulder that settled onto the sandy bottom. After a great struggle, she managed to twist around and kick the soft earth with both feet. She rose to the surface and filled her lungs with a long, liberating breath of air before two merciless hands thrust her head back down again. She struggled furiously, hitting the side of her head against a protruding nail as she tried to grab hold of one of the piles but still managing, twice in a row, to get her face up out of the water. Through the veil of her wet hair, she saw to her horror a fanatical gleam of determination in the eyes of her assailant looming over her. True to her literary instincts, even on the threshold of death, Gisèle Dambert was reminded absurdly of Katherine Mansfield's *The Fly* and realized that there would be no third surfacing. She was going to drown like the pitiful little insect pushed against its will to the bottom of the inkwell. For a moment she thought she heard a familiar voice shout her name, echoing as if from a long way off. Then she sank toward the black vortex of death by suffocation.

*

Shattering the icy silence of the surrounding countryside, Foucheroux's car screeched to a halt at the top of the embankment across from the gate to Mirougrain. In what

215

seemed like a single movement, he shut off the motor, jumped out of the car, and took two running leaps before collapsing onto the stubbly grass in unbearable pain. One of the steel pins that held his artificial knee in place had given way, and he lay nailed to the cold, wet ground like a panting and disjointed jumping jack. "Run, Leila, run," he shouted as she rushed over to help him. "Gisèle Dambert . . . Quick, Leila . . ."

She hesitated for just a moment, wiped the sympathy that she knew he would find intolerable from her eyes, and dashed off toward the watery surface below. Guided by a faint rustling noise and then by the gurgling sounds of someone gasping for air, she came up to the bank of the pond across from the Mirougrain grounds and, adjusting her stride to the distance remaining, took a running jump that landed her safely on the other bank. In the shadows, she could just make out the silhouette of a man squatting down on a rotting wood pontoon, who seemed to be dunking a ball into the water.

"Police! Hands up!" she called out, drawing her pistol.

The figure rose up immediately and reached for his right-hand pocket.

"Hands up!" she said again, with all the authority her voice could muster. She saw what looked like a glimmer of metal. Gisèle's face, twisted with fear, flashed before her mind's eye. She took aim at the man's leg and fired. As the shot rang out, he staggered. Hit square in the heart, he fell like a stone into the black pool, his hand still clutching Gisèle's long, dripping hair.

Just as Leila dived into the still rippling water, the broad yellow headlights of an ambulance, its siren blaring through the night, cast their harsh light over the brown water of the pond and the white froth floating on its surface.

*

I'm cold, Gisèle said to herself, struggling feebly to pull up the covers of the bed where she was curled up in an artificially induced slumber. "I'm cold," she said out loud, still unable to open her eyes. It felt as though her eyelids were glued to her cheeks with yellow wax. "I'm cold," she said again. As if she had spoken some magic formula, a round, solemn-looking face under a white cap appeared above her, and a practiced hand took her by the wrist to feel her pulse.

"Are we awake now?" the young nurse said in a professional tone. "You're at Chartres Hospital. Everything's going to be fine."

"Everything's going to be fine?" Gisèle asked worriedly as she felt a needle pierce her left arm. She remembered someone's mouth on hers, hands pushing rhythmically against her chest, a plastic mask placed over her nose and mouth, and the first words that penetrated her consciousness. Victorious words. "She's alive."

"I'm alive," she thought joyfully.

And in the impersonal sterility of the hospital room, illuminated in spots by a silvery, wavering moon, she fell into a deep and peaceful sleep.

24

THE NEXT MORNING the village, immured in a continual drizzle, was abuzz with the most fantastic rumors about the violent deeds that had upset the nocturnal peace of the region. Everyone had his own theory, and the crowd in Mme Blanchet's grocery was growing thicker every minute. One of the most widely spread rumors had it that the secretary had murdered her boss and then gone off, in the throes of remorse, to drown herself in the Mirougrain pond, but had been fished out in extremis by M. Desforge, whom the police had shot and killed by accident. Another hypothesis held that "foreign agents" had fomented a conspiracy to ruin the reputation of Aunt Léonie's as a place of literary pilgrimage in order to recover the enormous sums embezzled by the late president.

Despite the weather a throng of journalists had descended on the village and were standing, recorders in hand, cameras rolling, in the middle of the streets, in cafés, and at shop entrances to "interview" all the inhabitants who had had even the remotest connection to the

"Proust Case." The unchallenged star of the day was the cleaning woman who had discovered one of the bodies. A camera crew from Channel Ten had besieged her little house on the banks of the Loir to depict "a special day in the life of Émilienne Robichoux" and were arguing, in a friendly confusion of languages, over who would get to do an exclusive interview with Ray Taylor's film team.

The bakers had wisely tripled their daily production of madeleines and brioches. One of them had been astute and audacious enough to get rid of his unsold wares from the day before by cleverly putting up a sign: "Biscottes and Toast from the Proust Manuscripts."

Aunt Léonie's was closed, but the indefatigable André Larivière had organized several bus tours at a moment's notice in collaboration with the Tourist Office. It was as though Mme Bertrand-Verdon's death, followed by that of her assassin, had exorcized all the old antipathies and replaced them with a unanimous spirit of goodwill and a bittersweet satisfaction at the idea that justice had been done.

*

Leila Djemani had spent the night prostrate on the floor of her hotel room. For the second time she had had to choose between one person's life and another's. For the second time she had found herself in the position of supreme judge. . . . For the thousandth time, she told herself she would have to change her career if she didn't learn to better absorb the job's psychological aftershocks.

A gray dawn was just beginning to work its way through the opening in the imperfectly closed curtains of the window that faced onto the back of the hotel when the phone rang.

219

"Detective Djemani? I'm writing up the report," Foucheroux said in a voice that showed no particular emotion. "I was wondering if you would like to give me a hand, and whether a cup of Colombian coffee would be a sufficient bribe."

"Give me ten minutes," she said, realizing immediately that he must not have slept either, having to brave both an almost unbearable physical pain on top of the still less tolerable feeling of failure.

When she had last seen him, she was dripping muddy water in all directions and he was half seated, half prostrate at the edge of a sunken lane, looking utterly vulnerable. A nurse was urging him vainly to let them carry him to the ambulance on a stretcher. His feeble attempt at joviality ("You look just like the Lady of the Lake!") was belied by his face, which was uncontrollably contorted with pain.

"Philippe Desforge is dead." It was all she seemed capable of saying.

"But Gisèle Dambert is alive," he shot back. "You saved her life."

"Yes," she concurred after a moment. "We saved her life."

"Not we, Leila. You. You saved her life." He looked away. "I'm sorry," he said. "I'm terribly sorry. . . ." He paused for a long moment. "I guess I should resign."

At that point her nerves snapped and she went into a violent rage, a reaction that surprised both of them equally but which had a salutary effect on the situation, since it was her sympathy he had wanted most to avoid. And then he had refused to let them take him to the hospital, but she had gotten him to promise to call the surgeon who had operated on him three years earlier.

She knocked at his door and was greeted with a rather

220

gruff-sounding "It's open." He was propped up in a wing chair with a laptop computer, a cup of coffee by his side.

"Help yourself," he said, pointing to a steaming pot of coffee on a hotplate next to him. "Are you ready to hear my account?"

She nodded and sat down on the armchair facing his, after dropping a lump of sugar into her cup.

"The most fascinating element in this case," he began, "is the victim. She made the strongest impression on everyone she met. You either loved her or you hated her, but there was no middle ground. We'll never know what drove her to want always to stand out, to be forever in the spotlight, to put everyone else in the shadows, but there's no doubt that she wanted all of this, and that she had worked out a plan guaranteed to open the doors of academe — both in France and in America, it seems — and assure her of an unassailable position at the heart of the provincial aristocracy. Patrick Rainsford, Guillaume Verdaillan, and the Viscount of Chareilles were in her mind nothing but pawns, and she pushed them in whatever direction she pleased. She was willing to employ any means under the sun to further her ends: bribery, blackmail, sex . . . On the eve of the convention she had at last achieved what she wanted, total control of everyone around her. But she hadn't counted on the effects of one very human emotion: jealousy."

He paused to finish his cup of coffee. Leila waited for him to continue.

"As sure as I am that the attempt on Gisèle Dambert's life was premeditated, so sure am I that Adeline Bertrand-Verdon's death was the result of an accident. Philippe Desforge had discovered that she was about to announce her engagement to M. de Chareilles and put her name next to that of Guillaume Verdaillan on the edition of Proust's works, the publication of which he could not afford to put off. His whole future was at stake. He must have realized in a flash how Adeline had been using him over the last several months. He had divorced his wife to be with her and had gone out on a limb for her at Martin-Dubois Press. They had never quite been able to forgive him the publication of the *Guide of the Perfect Proustian,* which had hurt the reputation of the house and been the laughingstock of the critics, and here she was sending him back into the fray once more, forcing him to defend an editorial decision that he knew was absurd. This time she had gone too far.

"He must have used a pretext urgent enough to get her to come immediately to Aunt Léonie's on the night of the crime. She wasn't planning on going out again, just on phoning Patrick Rainsford and Guillaume Verdaillan to make sure that the jaws of her various traps were all set to close on their respective victims. She went up to her room, ate two spoonfuls of her habitual rose-petal jam — unaware that Gisèle Dambert had spiked it with soporific — and was just getting ready for bed when the telephone rang. We can only guess at the content of that conversation. Did Philippe Desforge disguise his voice and threaten to reveal the truth about her divorce unless she came to Aunt Léonie's right that minute? Or did he tell her she had to come and talk with him if she was really counting on coediting Proust's complete works with Professor Verdaillan? Did he think up something else? Whatever he said, it frightened Adeline enough that she rushed to the meeting that had been forced upon her, forgetting everything in her panic but her keys!"

The image of an animal at bay appeared suddenly in Leila's mind. In retrospect she felt a kind of disapproving

222

pity at the idea of Adeline finding herself caught in her own trap.

"Their fight must have been appalling," Jean-Pierre Foucheroux went on. "How did she react to him when she got there? How many times must he have begged her to change her mind? We'll never know. But I'm guessing that in the end, she found some means of humiliating him. The little statue of the bathing girl was standing on the desk where Théodore had put it earlier that day. In a fit of jealous anger, Philippe Desforge grabbed hold of it and struck Adeline while she was deriding him."

"And he was wearing his gloves," Leila said, "which is why we didn't find his fingerprints —"

"He was indeed wearing his gloves, to hide the rash that had so horribly blemished his hands. But then he wanted to make sure that Adeline Bertrand-Verdon was really dead, and he took them off and put his fingers directly onto the victim's neck and wrist to feel for her pulse, leaving the traces of desquamation that the autopsy report mentions —"

"But why did he go after Gisèle Dambert?" Leila asked.

"Doubtless because she was the only person alive who could ruin his career any time she pleased: she owned the notebooks."

"But the notebooks had been stolen by a group of Italian tourists, at least according to Professor Verdaillan. . . ."

"There are still a few cloudy issues that can be cleared up, I'm sure, by a brief visit to Mlle Dambert. Strangely, after committing his dire deed, Philippe Desforge never lost his head. He had just murdered the woman of his dreams, but he could still save his career. He wanted to make us believe he was on his way back to Paris at the moment when Gisèle Dambert, crippled with remorse, was drowning herself in the pond. Let's stop by the Chartres

223

Hospital on the way back to Paris and look in on her. All we have to do before we leave is thank Sergeant Tournadre for his splendid work and finish up the final version of our report. We should have everything done by ten. I'd like to be at the Quai des Orfèvres by noon. Charles Vauzelle is expecting us."

Leila got up. "About last night —," she began.

"Not another word about it," he said. "I've got an appointment at Cochin Hospital this afternoon. If only all wounds were as easy to sew up as an artificial knee! And Leila, about Philippe Desforge —"

"Not another word about it," she said, cutting him off without the shadow of a smile.

And she walked out.

*

Patrick Rainsford had gotten up at dawn and, elated to learn that all danger had passed, somewhat rashly accepted Professor Verdaillan's invitation to breakfast.

In the end it was just as well he had. Over a croissant and a slice of bread and jam he managed to extract several valuable pieces of information from his colleague, not the least of which concerned the young Dambert, apparently one of the rising stars of Proustian studies. "One of the major players of the next generation, without a doubt," Verdaillan assured him. "And in the current climate, it doesn't hurt that she's a woman," he added, pursing his lips as though his coffee had suddenly turned bitter.

As soon as he had paid his hotel bill, Patrick Rainsford drove to Chartres, where he had no difficulty finding the hospital in which Gisèle Dambert, alone in her room, had just been awakened by a nurse bringing her an enormous bouquet of flowers bearing a card with the following message:

> With my best wishes for a rapid recovery, and in eager anticipation of the pleasure of hearing you defend our thesis,
>
> Sincerely,
> Professor Verdaillan

In spite of the medication encumbering her thought, Gisèle knew immediately what the message really meant: her doctoral advisor thought the deal was still on. She would keep quiet about the notebooks. He would make sure she was called to his chair at the University of Paris at Neuilly when he retired in two years. She closed her eyes, too exhausted to think about what she was going to do. The noise of a dispute in the hallway shook her from her torpor, and a smiling, impeccably groomed Patrick Rainsford burst into her room.

"So, Mlle Dambert, I hear you're doing better."

"Somewhat," she admitted.

"I don't mean to disturb you, but I didn't want to leave without seeing you again. I have a proposition for you. . . ."

Astonished, the young woman listened as he "proposed" she transform her doctoral thesis into an American Ph.D. and that she assume as of next January the vice-presidency of the Center for Postmodern Manuscripts at a very prestigious university on the East Coast of the United States. He needed a geneticist. . . . The salary would be quite comfortable and she would be housed, without charge, of course, at Hansford House for as long as she pleased. . . .

"I'm very . . . honored by your offer," she said when he

had finished. "I'll write to you as soon as I'm well enough to make a decision."

Patrick Rainsford was about to insist when a nurse threatened to notify her supervisor if he remained another two seconds in a patient's room outside visiting hours.

An hour later a discreet knock at the door announced the arrival of Inspector Foucheroux and Detective Djemani. "They look terrible," she thought when she saw them, oblivious to her own frightful pallor. Leila had wide dark circles under her eyes, the corners of which were pulled down by her sagging cheeks, giving her a kind of false Asian appearance. Jean-Pierre Foucheroux limped wretchedly over to her bed. Gisèle suggested he sit down and prop his leg up on a chair, and to her great surprise, he obeyed without a word.

"I can imagine you don't feel much like answering a thousand different questions, Mlle Dambert. But there are one or two cloudy issues only you can help us to clear up," he said gently. "Do you feel strong enough to do that?"

"If it doesn't take too long," she said simply. But in fact it was a great relief to be able, finally, to tell the whole truth: Évelyne's gift, Adeline Bertrand-Verdon's duplicity, the particulars of her own plan to get her stolen notebooks back, the visit to the Teissandier farm, her conversation with Philippe Desforge, who had decided to kill her as soon as he realized that in the end she would never agree to the deal that Guillaume Verdaillan had proposed.

"We won't ask you how you got to the Old Mill Inn and then to Paris and to Mme Bertrand-Verdon's apartment on the night of the crime," said Inspector Foucheroux. "It doesn't matter now —"

"You're right," she said, "it doesn't matter now. I'm going to America."

He raised his eyebrows, which made him look as though he were disappointed to hear the news.

"America?"

"Yes. Professor Rainsford has offered me a job. I think I'm going to accept." She was about to say, "Has anyone ever told you that you look like the vice president of the United States?" but she stopped herself just in time. She turned her gaze to Leila and held out her hand. "Thank you," she said.

"No need to thank me," Leila responded, rather more stiffly than was called for. "Take care of yourself, Mlle Dambert."

"And you take care of him," Gisèle said in a whisper. "Perhaps you'll come and visit me?" she added aloud.

"Why not?" Inspector Foucheroux said as he got up. "And as for the notebooks, I'm going to put my friend Blazy, in Cannes, to work on them straightaway. If anyone can find them, he can. I'll keep you posted, if you'll leave a forwarding address."

"I most certainly will," she said with a mischievous smile that made her look rather like a little girl. "And anyway, I owe you money."

When they had left, Gisèle turned on her side and closed her eyes. She didn't want to think about Yvonne or about Selim. It was no concern of hers, now. She no longer wanted to die for a man who had been her type. She'd already lost enough time. She only wondered how Katicha would react when she told her that they were going to be moving abroad. . . .

*

227

In Illiers-Combray, Émilienne's moment of glory had passed. She had gotten as much mileage as possible out of her recollections of what had happened two days before, and her picture had appeared on the front page of all the local newspapers. She was busy cooking up a tasty stew for Ferdinand, the game warden, who, after a lot of hemming and hawing, had accepted her invitation to dinner. Émilienne couldn't help smiling when she imagined the expression on his sister's face when she heard where he was going. The two women had been enemies since grade school. She mixed a handful of herbs into her stew, the effects of which had been proven through centuries of white magic. Then she adjusted her hair, took off her apron, and put a bottle of Muscadet on the table. Tonight, Jeanne was likely to wait a long time for her brother to come home, a very long time.